John Hill

The Waters of Marah

Vol. II

John Hill

The Waters of Marah
Vol. II

ISBN/EAN: 9783337053345

Printed in Europe, USA, Canada, Australia, Japan

Cover: Foto ©Andreas Hilbeck / pixelio.de

More available books at **www.hansebooks.com**

THE

WATERS OF MARAH.

A Novel.

BY

JOHN HILL.

Farewell and adieu !
Each year that we live shall we sing it anew
With a water untravelled before us for sailing,
And a water behind us that wrecks may bestrew.

IN THREE VOLUMES.

VOL. II.

LONDON:
TINSLEY BROTHERS, 8, CATHERINE STREET, STRAND.
1883.

CHARLES DICKENS AND EVANS,
CRYSTAL PALACE PRESS.

CONTENTS.

Part the Third.—Caspar's Midsummer M ss.

(Continued.)

CHAPTER III. *(continued.)*

PAGE

DICK MENTEITH 3

CHAPTER IV.

CASPAR ANALYZES HIMSELF 15

CHAPTER V.

CASPAR'S DREAMING 47

CONTENTS.

Part the Fourth.—A Lost Sheep of the House of Israel.

CHAPTER I.

PAGE

MRS. BRANDON 65

CHAPTER II.

THE RETURN JOURNEY 85

CHAPTER III.

DICK'S DREAMING 103

CHAPTER IV.

JESSICA STUDIES THE RÔLE OF ATE 118

CHAPTER V.

DICK STUDIES TWO PICTURES 148

CHAPTER VI.

IN ILLYRIA AGAIN 172

𝔓art the 𝔉ifth.—𝔐arriage and 𝔇eath and 𝔇ivision.

CHAPTER I.

PAGE

WEDDING MARCH 199

CHAPTER II.

THE DUTCH DEVIL 219

CHAPTER III.

A FRIENDLY ALLIANCE 241

THE WATERS OF MARAH.

Part the Third.
(*Continued.*)

CASPAR'S MIDSUMMER MADNESS.

THE WATERS OF MARAH.

CHAPTER III. (*continued*).

DICK MENTEITH.

HERE Caspar and Dick Menteith reached the front terrace of the castle, which overhung the river valley, a terrace of red stone, which Kimburls persisted in calling a "bolcony.' And Caspar said, "Come and look over the parapet." And they leaned on the broad balustrade with their elbows, and looked up and down, right and left. Below, dark green depths, shaded by heavy hanging ivy, cooled by minute cataracts gliding over mossy miniature precipices. In front, and far below, the river

Schlange brown and bright, with an endless timber-raft struggling sinuously through an arch of the town bridge, and on the other river-bank the white, hot road, winding along the base of the Traubenberg, with its façade of hanging gardens, new villas, and old taverns, above the red, sloping, buttressed wall. To the right, the brown-tiled house-tops and red spires of the town, which the evening sun was shining on for the last few minutes of the day. Far away over the fog-laden plain beyond, the factory chimneys stood up, and sent their thin, straight streaks of brown smoke athwart the lines of misty crimsoning western sky. To the left, the dark, steep-sided, tree-clad river valley wound out of sight, growing momentarily dimmer and duller. Neither of the two spoke for some time, for what they saw and felt was far more than any words of theirs could then express ; and inspirations and spontaneous eloquence deserted them. At last Dick said :

" Will I see anything in Dresden better than this ? "

Caspar looked at her for a moment, and replied :

" No. After all, I don't believe you will, or anywhere else either." This broke the spell of silence, and Caspar continued : " Where did you get your enthusiasm for nature and mediævalism ? If I may say so without rudeness, I don't think you inherited it."

" I live in Scotland."

" Well ? "

" The only books I have had to read that I cared for were old books, old histories, old ballads, and Sir Walter Scott. I really think the most modern author I have read is the Ettrick Shepherd."

" Don't you read the modern nineteenth-century novel ? "

"I have read some. I like them when they are good ; but I don't like many."

"That remark implies a minor premiss uncomplimentary to the books."

"Oh, it does that !" Curiously enough, Caspar did not find the slight and rather plaintive Scotch accent, which was undeniably, though inconspicuously, present in Dick Menteith, either ridiculous or irritating, though the manner of speech of her father and aunt frequently gave him both those impressions. But there was nothing ridiculous or irritating about this quiet, small, white figure in a crowning straw hat, leaning on the wide red-stone balustrade, and gazing into the far-off sky.

" Do you write books ? " said she, turning her face Casparward.

"I have co-operated in producing a play once, and have written songs and stories in magazines. I never wrote a novel. I may some day, though I doubt if either public or publisher would like it."

" Why ? "

"You see the matter between the public and me is this. It is very simple. I don't like them, and those that know me, or think they do, seldom like me. We should say disagreeable things to one another. It may be my misfortune, and it may be theirs; but I have an immense faculty for disliking people—perhaps the only strong and thorough faculty I have. It would command Dr. Johnson's robust respect, no doubt. But critics and librarians are not Dr. Johnsons —at least, not as a rule."

" But I don't see why one would dislike people ? "

" No. You are not one who would very readily provoke, or feel hatred or contempt. I hope you will remain always in that mind."

" Are you not happy ? "

Caspar resisted the temptation to say that he was at that moment particularly happy, and replied :

"Not always. I am informed by those who consider themselves judges, that I have a morbid temperament, because I tell the truth as it seems to me — namely, that human beings on the average are very mean animals, and that I'm one of them. I have been rather prejudiced perhaps by the eccentricities of Fate in my own particular experiences."

"I think you're just a little proud of that 'morbid temperament,' as you call it."

"Don't suppose I'm affecting an opinion or playing a part ; I should have no purpose in doing that. I mean what I say. Perhaps I am a little proud of my discoveries ; they are as worthy being proud of as many other things which are held to justify pride. However, never mind pride and misanthropy and meanness; they are not savoury subjects when we are looking from the Schloss of old Schlangenberg into the evening red. Tell me what you are thinking of?" (This last rather suddenly.)

Dick turned her eyes again on Caspar's. "It is difficult to know whether one thinks at all in a scene like this. At any rate, it is not very speakable."

These were the words of her mouth. The meditation of her heart, which Caspar read in her eyes, was, "I am thinking of you." (Long pause.)

"Well, Dick," said George Farringdon, "have you discovered anything in infinite space?"

"I am not very sure."

"Jolly view, isn't it?" observed Farringdon carelessly to Caspar.

"Awfully jolly," returned that individual drily, with a perfectly untranslatable face.

Dick was not quite sure what she had discovered in the purpling region of the west ; nor was she quite sure why she felt just a little annoyed with George for his slightly unexpected and inopportune observations.

But she had no time to speculate on these questions, as the party reunited, and the conversation became general, modern, and every-day, the voice of Kimburls being dominant. Dick spoke little, and coiled a shawl round her neck and shoulders with a little shiver, as they turned their backs on the terrace, and all it looked upon, and found themselves in the darkness of the wood, where the fire-flies were chasing one another among the leaves. When the town outskirts were reached, Caspar said he must withdraw, and Charlie, of course, took the cue.

On shaking hands, Dick said to Caspar,

" Will we see you again to-morrow ? " in a
rather low voice. Why she should ask such
a harmless question in a low, rather than a
loud voice, she did not entirely know.

But Caspar thought he did, and said:
" Yes, you may be sure of that."

And he and Charlie strode away into
the town, and lost themselves in the narrow
lanes till they found themselves outside an
old tavern, at a secluded corner of a tall
narrow street. This Caspar led the way
into, and ordered supper, while through the
open windows on the opposite side of the
street came the joyous chant, "*Ich lobe mir
das alte Burschen leben,*" from a club of
uproarious students.

While waiting for supper, Charlie tried
to spell out the jokes from the *Fliegender
Blätter*, and Caspar leaned out at the
window, regarding the street below and the
stars above. And he was happier than he

had ever been before in his life, as he reflected: "And I can read the fairy-tales in those eyes! Watch this town, you golden fires that fret the majestical roof of earth! It has more in it than beer and stupidity. It contains the girl I shall always love, and who shall always love me. I know it; I can make her; I can reveal it to her.

Let come what will, there is one thing worth
To have had fair love in the life upon earth:
While skies had colour——"

"Here's the supper, old man!"

They ate with appetite and contentment.

"Do you mean to cut out Farringdon?" asked Charlie carelessly, at the end of their meal.

"Cut—out—Farringdon? As how?"

"Ah, I see! Well, the sooner I enlighten you the better, as you seem to take an unusual interest in this matter. George

Farringdon is engaged to Miss Dick Menteith, and has been so for the last six or eight months."

Caspar sat perfectly still, leaning forward on his elbows on the table, and looking straight before him into Charlie's face.

"I did not know it," he replied shortly. "I thought he wanted to be, but not that he was."

"I thought I'd better tell you."

"Quite right. Let's pay and go."

And they walked home.

In the night Caspar rose silently and went for a long walk under the starlight, through the woods to the hill-top above the town, where

> The air with sparks of living fire was spangled,
> And night, deep-drenched in misty Acheron,
> Heaved up her head, and half the world upon
> Breathed darkness forth.

The cold crimson dawn had arisen over

the river valley when he came down. Then
he lay on his bed, and after throwing a book
on the floor he had sought some few futile
minutes' solace from, remained there on his
back watching through the open attic-window
the first sunshine on the distant façade of the
time-worn ruin on the misty mountain-side.
There were streaks of crimson and pearly
layers on a vivid green eastern atmosphere.
Then the nightingale's voice became dumb,
and the noisy tramp and traffic of the flower
and vegetable market far below began. And
Caspar stood at his window watching. Far to
his right and below, in the balcony of the
hotel in the same square, he saw the fair
sunlit little head of Dick Menteith. She
was looking at the same sunrise, and at the
same blue-print market-women in ceaseless
movement.

CHAPTER IV.

Behüet dich Gott! Es wär' zu schön gewesen,
Behüet dich Gott! Es hat nicht sollen sein.

CASPAR spent the morning of the next day in fierce perturbed discussion with himself, in keen analysis of his rather obscure and indeterminate position, and in making and unmaking resolves as to what he was to say or do.

A couple of hours' silent smoking after breakfast in the garden, accompanied by strides up and down that limited tract of land, did little to reduce the spiritual Maëlstrom which had occupied the place of a mind in him ever since that well-intended but epoch-marking statement of Charlie's.

The latter young man, when tired of the exciting adventures of James, Mr. M., and the daughters of the merchant, as portrayed in the work which professed to teach him German without a master, looked up at Caspar with a curious, amused, and withal wistful eye, through what he (Charlie) termed the Monocle of the Higher Criticism ; and after studying him for some minutes in profound silence, observed :

"You had better sit down and talk. It will be better for you to do that than to roam up and down like a confined arboreal ancestor."

"What ?" said the other suddenly, turning on his heel.

"If you want the advantage of my advice and sympathy, you had better tell me your symptoms."

" Peace! Thou talkest of nothing, and dost mightily drivel withal."

" I was talking of you from the point of view of your medical adviser and asylum-keeper."

"Yes. That's particularly brilliant as con-versation. Have you much more of that kind of thing to say ? "

" Goodness! The man is trying to be disagreeable, and doesn't know how. In sober earnest, man, leave off that silent rambling ; I can't stand it. If things aren't exactly square between us, well, they ought to be made so, *quam celerrime*, or what's the use of anything, you know ? "

" It is curious to notice how your usually incisive and coherent style of talk degenerates when you are in what you call earnest."

" Well then, look here ; have I done you any harm ? "

" Not that you know of."

"Then why the devil do you snub me when I try to be pleasant? That's coherent, I think."

"I beg your pardon; I was ill-tempered and unpleasant. I was only looking on you as an impersonal object to (spiritually) throw things at. Anyone else would do."

"All right; I understand. I fancy I've been there myself. Usual routine, I suppose? Insomnia, incoherent ravings when alone, strong susceptibility to lunar and biliary affections?"

"Quite so. Patient displays great mental acerbity when not alone, tending to relieve itself in violent deeds or remarks on the nearest inoffensive object—so look out; sees faces—particularly one face; has an exaggerated craving for tobacco, a diminished appetite for all meaner things; feels an exalted contempt alternately for the human race and for himself, together with a sullen silence, or undignified tendency to unpack his heart with words which are profitless; progress from bad to worse."

" And he has also a feeble and transparent jocularity."

" Yes. D——d funny, isn't it ? "

" Look here, man, you've got it bad. Excuse my slang. Don't try to be funny, and sit down and say in plain English, what do you mean to do ? "

"In plain English, my view of the situation is this: Here is a girl who is not sufficiently experienced to know that she does not yet know her own mind, although she has made it up to marry a man—a man whom I do not highly appreciate, but who does not appear to be particularly unworthy, though he is distinguished neither for great learning nor great taste. That is, he might make a very pleasant and serviceable comrade for her, as you say he has been her friend and companion from infancy, etc."

"That's all very well as far as it goes; but you know, to put it with due regard to truth, you are worth any fifty of George M. Farringdon, as the Americans would call him, and she, if she's the girl I think she is, could be fonder of you than she ever will be of him."

"That may or may not be," replied Caspar through his set teeth, again beginning his quarter-deck stride. "The question is, have I any right, under the circumstances, to try to make her take that view of the matter? Of course the common vulgar Don Juan joke doesn't come in here. I should fail to see the point of such jokes about this girl in particular —in fact, they would annoy me considerably. Do the facts justify me in supposing that it would be better for her, or worse, if I were to place myself in antagonism to this young man? Whether it would be better or worse for him, or me, we will provisionally set aside."

"I should say the facts were very simple indeed. Here is a girl—a nice girl. Two men want her. One is of a higher class in the animal kingdom than the other. Evolution and common generosity say, 'Give her the best.'"

"Interpreting that in the flattering sense you intend, I still say you omit important factors on both sides, if I may treat this kind of thing as a sort of quadratic equation. You forget that she knows this fellow well, and likes him; that she has been brought up with certain ideas, comforts, and habits of life, traditions he may partially keep up, luxuries he may be able to increase, society he can move in; all of which things are not to be found in me. On the other side, she probably guesses but faintly, if at all, that my notions on many subjects dear to her may be very different from her own, and repulsive to her; or that my life is one of hand-to-mouth income, hard work, and rather Illyrian amusements and society. You couldn't offer her a bar-room, and call it society, could you? And I don't just now know of any other I could take her into. I could only offer her a share in the profits of my magnificent genius, which brings in just enough to keep one body inside clothes and outside food. Besides, I should have to try and persuade her to act in defiance of her family. You realise the meaning of that, I suppose? Well, having no compensation except my interesting person to offer in return for a lower life and estranged family, strange ways and notions, and highly probable ultimate work-house, with boys selling special editions, and girls penny bunches of violets, looming before us, without the fortune that is dug up in the seventh tableau of a melodrama coming with redemption in its hands, I say, No.

I daren't ask her to face all that, even in a dream, and she is not expecting me to ask her."

"But supposing she takes a liking to you, whether you choose or not? Such things have been; and mere flight on your part would then be too late."

"Doing that kind of thing would only serve to accentuate the (hypothetical) present phase of her fancy, and stimulate her latent instincts into analytical activity."

"Very prettily put. What its precise connection with the plot is one sees. So lucid. And what might you interpret the present phase of her fancy, as you call it, to be?"

"Don't try to be sarcastic, young one; it doesn't suit you; you haven't got the vocabulary for it at your disposal, and it doesn't irritate me in the least."

"Oh, doesn't it? Then why that crushing reply? However, don't begin to argue. I know nothing about love and all that. By Jove! there's the postman!" And Charlie rushed to waylay the dignified, flat-capped, military-looking old man, who was spelling out English names on letters. There was one for Charles Deane, Esq., to which he paid great and agitated attention.

"Who is it from, Charlie? Anyone I know?"

"Lily."

"Oh! Anything in it?"

"Doosid little."

As there was extensive crossing visible on the large thin paper, which some people will persist in using, this statement seemed unaccountable. Caspar at length looked as if he had made his mind up to some course or other. His face brightened, his talk became more fluent and flippant, and he seemed to find more amusement in things that surrounded him than when in his former inly concentrated condition.

Charlie retired into the fastnesses of the fourth floor, where he was left undisturbed by Caspar, to re-read Lily Carew's letter, and to answer the same, which he did in the following manner :

"16, Ross-Platz, Schlangenberg.

" DEAR LILY,

"I got your letter to-day, and am grateful, though it is not exactly what I call interesting. There are several things I don't care twopence about, on which you give me full details, and several more which I care a good deal about, on which you say hardly anything. Never mind. Excuse my plainness (bother the phrase! I mean plain speech). As my dear old friend Otto's grammar would say, Charles has the bad pen, the muddy ink, the unsatisfactory letter, and the disturbed temper.

"The matter is that that dreadful old lunatic, C. Rosenfeld, has gone and fallen in love with Miss Dick Menteith; and she is in a fair way, if he makes an effort to accelerate her, towards the same condition with regard to C. R. The latter party has been wandering about the country like Lear and his fool, especially the latter, when he thought I was asleep and didn't know, and worshipping

> The dawn and the moon and the trees,
> And bogies and serpents and crows,

like primitive man, out of poetic despair. It's an awful shame to laugh at him, because it's really a great pity, and Lord only knows what will happen. I mean to prescribe *pot. bromide gr. xxv.* After a morning of argumentary nagging, and walking up and down the garden like a Barbary cat, he has arrived at a kind of cheerfully triumphant expression and a rather jocular style of conversation, so I presume that he is going to unmask his batteries and declare war with G. M. Farringdon, in which case I advise G. M. F. to look out. But how Caspar can support a wife when he gets her is beyond me. I hope it mayn't be equally beyond him.

"Tell me, when you write, all about yourself—what you are doing, reading, and thinking. I can't tell you how much I miss you here. I am sure you would enjoy such a jolly place as this is. Write soon— whatever you like, but write soon.—Your affectionate cousin,

"CHARLES DEANE."

This epistle Charlie stamped and took to the post at once. He usually posted his answers to Lily's letters half-an-hour after

they came, as clerks say, "to hand." She
usually began writing about ten days after
receiving his correspondence, and then forgot
to post her letter for a few days more. It
was her way, just as the opposite way was
his. Then he came back to Caspar, saying:
" Well, is it all right?"

"Yes, Charlie, it's all right. Where
shall we dine?" He did not mean to quote
Romeo.

In the afternoon Caspar and Charlie
performed their usual digestive tramp under
the chestnuts of the shady Anlage, where
Caspar railed a good deal on the German
corps-student, his ideas, his affectations, and
his amusements. After a while they met
Farringdon (everyone meets everyone else on
the Anlage), when Caspar suddenly changed
his tone completely, and began an eloquent
defence of the free life and unfettered mirth
of the German student, to Farringdon's con-

siderable disgust, as that gentleman held the
opinion, common to young Oxford and
Cambridge, that the *studiosus* of a German
university is invariably an object of both
pity and contempt. After listening to Caspar
for a few minutes, he said :

"I always regarded them as a set of
thorough cads. They certainly dress terribly. Don't they spend most of their leisure
time in drinking beer ? "

"Yes. Why not ? It is very good beer.
They enjoy it. So would you. Would you
not like to come to a *kneipe* just once in a
way, out of curiosity ? "

"How can I go ? "

"I can take you. I belong to a society
of students here. I am very fond of temporary dissipation, combined with good songs
and stories."

"You understand the awful language,
then ? "

"Oh, yes; after a fashion I understand several languages."

The three walked on together.

"You live in town, I suppose, when you are in England?"

"Yes. I oscillate between Barnard's Inn and the Strand."

"I suppose you literary and artistic men have rather a gay time of it—not much fettered by conventionality, eh?" Here George looked knowing.

Caspar looked knowing too, and repeated the impressive formula, "What do *you* think?" at which Farringdon laughed; and Charlie thought Caspar was really going mad.

"Are you in town much?" asked Caspar.

"I used to go down to town a good deal in the vacs. I have been in Scotland, and in my place down at Sokebridge lately."

"I was only wondering I hadn't met you anywhere at the places where men do meet—supper-rooms, bars, and stage-doors, for example. Remember the Duke's? Know Scott's?"

"Er—I have been there, I believe."

"Once—out of curiosity? Like me. Last time I was there I saw a charming young woman chasing ants round her plate with a knife. Of course there were no ants. Early in life, I thought, for that sort of thing."

"By Jove, you seem to take things calmly!"

"What's the use of taking them any other way? Give me life, and plenty of it, and the rest of the world can do and say what they please."

"You'll have to change all those ideas when you settle down like me, and marry."

"I? Settle down? No, sir. I prefer to sip my sweets selectively, at all times and places, unshackled by domestic ties. I have no relatives to speak of, and occupy myself studying humanity, especially in its female varieties, in the style of the experimentalist."

" Strikes me you're a devilish gay dog, you know, and you don't seem at all ashamed of it."

" Ashamed ?

> I say of shame, what is it ?
> Of virtue, we can miss it ;
> Of sin, we can but kiss it,
> And it's no longer sin."

And Caspar soon launched out into what Falstaff called "discreet stories."

After they had parted from Farringdon, Charlie asked :

" I say, are you cracked ? "

Caspar flicked a leaf with his stick.

" Only north-north-west. Show me a handsaw, and I will without difficulty identify it among a mob of hawks. '

"What did you want to go and make yourself out a dissipated boastful cad for? Above all to that fellow!"

"Why above all to that fellow?"

"Because he's safe to go and repeat and exaggerate it all to the Menteiths."

"Not quite all, I fancy. Still, supposing he does?"

"People always believe anything bad about other people sooner than anything good."

"Precocious cynic! And then?"

"And then! Why, it's enough to make the girl take a distrust—a disgust almost— at you. And, by Jove, considering the handle you've given that fellow, she wouldn't be far wrong, not knowing you more than she does."

"And if she did," replied Caspar through his teeth, with a sort of writhe, "were it not a consummation devoutly to be wished?"

Charlie was silent awhile, and then said :

"You are a howling maniac, old fellow! Quixote wasn't in it.   But it won't do. You'll never be able to keep it up."

"We shall see."

"Well, I wash my hands of it.   It's your business, and not mine; but I must say I'm sorry to see a good thing go wrong —'a beautiful world broken up,' as the fellow in 'Faust' says—just through your fantastic self-will.   It is such a pity!"

"*Kreuz! Donnerwetter!*   And doesn't it occur to you that I may be sorry, too, for the collapse of the fairest vision that ever crossed my mind's eye?   More sorry than it would be easy or profitable to express.

> We built a castle in the air,
>   In summer weather, you and I;
> The wind and sun were in your hair—
>   Gold hair against a sapphire sky.

You may be right—time will show.   God

help her, if it be so! Never mind. Talk of something else."

Naturally, at this invitation, Charlie maintained a dead silence. He could not chatter on passing trivialities while his mind was trying to master the extraordinary and, to him, most unnatural behaviour of his friend. Caspar could, and had most of the conversation to himself—which was a curious fact.

"I wonder if I forced or overdid it?" reflected he in the mean time. "It doesn't much matter if I did. That man would never have detected it."

Later in the day, when he and Charlie met the whole Menteith party in a garden where the Stadt-Orchester discoursed sweet sounds to the best of its ability, Caspar's behaviour was simply woful. He boasted like a Bursch of the amount of beer he could drink; he made jokes on religious topics, and cynical remarks on womankind; paid

occasional compliments to Dick Menteith of
a vapid and "flirtatious" description, and,
a thing which lowered him in his own esti-
mation more than aught else, he submitted
to the statements and dogmatisms of Kimburls and Farringdon on matters social, political, and artistic.   He gave anecdotes of
theatrical experiences behind the scenes, and
reminiscences of every tavern from St. Paul's
to Temple Bar, which presented him in the
light of an experienced Paul's Walker, or
bar-room loafer of the most debased description, who gave "straight tips."   It were
idle to attempt to describe the keen internal
torture it caused him to watch the effect of
this on his audience.   Dick was perfectly
bewildered, and scarcely knew what to think;
Miss Menteith was simply scandalised, and
Farringdon and Kimburls triumphant; while
Charlie—honest man !—felt more anger than
sorrow, and longed to shake his friend by

the collar, and kick Farringdon into infinite ether. You see Farringdon was revealed at his best to Caspar, who had no knowledge whatever of him beyond what he observed. And what he observed was a young man in the most exalted, pure, and perfect condition possible to such a young man ; for being really in love with a fair and pure young girl, he was by that fact raised above his normal level. Even a man of exceptional powers, yea, also of genius (neither of which descriptions applies, of course, to poor George), is in a higher, better, and altogether more efficient and attractive condition when in love than at any other time. He burns to excel, for the sake of, or at any rate in presence of, the woman, and that renders him independent of all other and baser tastes, desires, and motives for the time. "They say, base men being in love have then a nobility in their natures more than is native to them." Thus Caspar formed an essentially exaggerated estimate of Farringdon's qualities as a man and a gentleman. But even Caspar, with his terrible resolution to dash his bark on the rocks before he had time to become sick and weary of the voyage, could not avoid an occasional breakdown, a lapse to his real self from the part he affected. And the worst, and to his mind most fatal, that occurred was this.

The conversation had got as far as Shakespeare, after travelling through multifarious preliminary channels of the musical glass order. Caspar was first of all irritated to find Kimburls and Farringdon cordially agreeing with him on some commonplace opinions he had expressed, and that loosened the high-pressure control in which he was holding his just then highly susceptible and irritable nervous system. Then the question came, "Was Hamlet really mad?" from Dick. Kimburls said, "I thought that was universally admitted. To give you my bonnafeedy opinion, that's a play I do not really prefer to read myself." Miss Menteith the elder knew that William Shakespeare was a play-actor, and there her knowledge ceased and the bard's condemnation began.

Farringdon was bound to put in a voice from the cultured academic and oracular circle he frequented, who read and talked about Shakespeare, misspelt his name, and read him very little, if at all; so he said: "The sublime madman of Elsinore was always a favourite character with me. One feels a strange subtle sympathy with his doubts, hesitations, and difficulties. Of course he was mad; I never heard the contrary seriously maintained. What do you think, Rosenfeld? you are a dramatic man, I think?"

"Looking at the recognised symptoms of his insanity, his killing such a wise and harmless counsellor, such an ideal father, as

Polonius, his subsequent unfeeling remarks, his brawling irreverence at a funeral, his brutal conversation with Ophelia——"

"Then you agree that he was mad ? " said Kimburls and Farringdon in one voice.

Caspar looked despairingly round him like a detected criminal, caught Dick's eyes fixed on him with a mournful curiosity, and drinking in his words—she knew her Shakespeare well, better than any but himself in the company—and suddenly all his great resolves to be insincerely commonplace fell with a crash, and he said slowly, with the flame of a forlorn hope shuddering through his eyes :

"Looking at all these things, I think the theory of Hamlet's madness perhaps the foremost among the many idiotic Shakespearean theories which weary and worry the world."

There was an expression of relief in Dick's

face, and one of stern satisfaction on Caspar's as he rose to take his leave. He and Charlie went away.

After they had gone, George said :

" I believe half that fellow's conversation is just swagger, you know."

" Which half, I wonder ? " said Kimburls.

" Oh, I don't pretend to understand the man myself. You hear all he says about himself, and you know what I told you."

As Caspar and Charlie walked away into the dark, leaving the music and mirth of the Palmen-Garten farther and farther behind, Charlie made one last appeal.

" It's too bad, Caspar ; I can't stand it— it's like suicide."

" My dear boy, I can't stand it myself ; I miscalculated my own powers. Look here, if you don't mind, we will leave here to-morrow, and roam about on foot a little in the Black Forest, or somewhere. I would like to be away among woods and mountains, where we can be alone; where there are no English tourist hotels, and where there is nothing to remind one of this place. It is to me the most beautiful place on the face of the earth, and I shall come back to it again some day years hence, when it has simply become as a grave that one visits, but I can't look at it now."

"All right. But——"

"Now, don't argue. I know my own mind. Don't talk to me about it just now, or I shall not be quite sure if I have a mind at all. I give her up—all chance of her—to him, because I think it seems best for her; but if he fails to make it best for her, then—— But I don't threaten, or go about hating and cursing people. I may kill him, all the same. I'm talking an immense deal too much, as it is. I don't want to bore you, old man; but Richard has not quite recovered his identity yet. I think you had better go to the Herrn Kleider-Macher in the Hauptstrasse, and ask him to call and measure me for a strait-waistcoat."

"Well, on the whole, I think I had."

"Ah, it will be all right by-and-by, when our summer in Schlangenberg becomes a ' dream of what was and no more is.' "

"I am not so sure of that, as far as you are concerned. One doesn't always wake up from these dreams as soon as one could wish."

"How do you know? Nightmares of the mind don't last longer than the intellectual indigestion which causes them. What's the time?"

"Bed-time; it's between eleven and twelve."

"Very good. We go at 8.40 to-morrow evening."

Long afterwards, poring at night alone

over that terrible scene of supreme sacrifice
and disappointment, in which Hamlet says,
"You should not have believed me—I loved
you not," Dick thought she understood, just
between herself and Shakespeare and the stars,
what it all meant. But she did not understand yet; she was only puzzled. She was
not angry with Caspar, as her father and
aunt were, nor did she deride him, as her
bridegroom did, in a way that almost
suggested personal malice or envy on his part.

But late that night, when they were
standing together in the hotel balcony, George
and she—he smoking cigarettes, she trying
to distinguish the different colours of the
stars, he noticed that she suddenly shivered,
in spite of the extremely high temperature of
the still, thunder-laden, summer night; and
George said:

"Hullo, what's the row with you, little
woman?"

"I don't know. I feel as if someone a long way off had just died."

"Cheerful! Look here, you're getting nervous, or hysterical, or something. Have some wine."

"No. But listen, George. Let us be married soon. Don't think that a very strange or silly thing for a girl to say."

George looked at her curiously, and replied:

"All right; sooner the better, I think." He dared not say "Why?"

And below, in the square, covered by the shadows of the chestnut-trees, stood a pale tall man, looking up into that bright soft yellow light, intersected by the iron tracery and creeping plants of the balcony, and the two figures which stood on it. And gentle intermittent flashes of summer lightning, low down on the horizon, made the scene flicker and expand and contract before his eyes, like a vertiginous dream; and he said to himself:

"Now, I wonder whether I have done an act of heroic renunciation, as poor Charlie thinks, or made myself ridiculous, to gratify an insane scruple, as I dimly surmise? It's one or the other; but I'm hanged if I know which.   Good-bye, *du reine schöne, holde!* There never were days like these, and there never will be again."

CHAPTER V.

There's something in his soul,
O'er which his melancholy sits on brood.
He shall with speed to England.

At 8.40 the next day a long train carried
Caspar and Charlie, in the moonlit twilight
of July, slowly—so slowly as only a German
express can go—across the level plain and
fertile fields that lay beyond the *débouchement*
of the Schlange valley. Caspar sat gazing
silently through the open window at the
mountains, which were darkening and dis-
appearing in the night and distance. He
looked at the last tall pinnacle of the red
roofless ruin overpeering the fir-tops, with the
eyes of one who knows that he sees for the

last time for many years the scene of the shortest and sweetest hours of a hard and wearisome life, and is on his way to a wearier weariness again, made more bitter by the vision of what might have made it sweet. Of course he was a fool, it will be said. Perhaps he was. At any rate he did not deny it. In that respect he deserves the sympathy of a goodly majority of human units.

And so Caspar Rosenfeld turned his back and fled, carrying with him a deathless memory of two calm gray eyes gazing into a summer evening, made up of great fiery golden wings of sunset clouds, which lost in the wind stray gleaming feathers and flakes wherewith the green-blue north-west became flecked as with little flames. Such was the scene in which he said a decorous society good-bye to Dick Menteith. Farringdon forgave him his Shakespearean criticism, and asked him to the approaching wedding at Sokebridge Manor.

And then Caspar went to summon a *Dientsmann* to carry his portmanteau.

> Beyond the glades,
> On the fir-forest, border, and the rim
> Of the low range of mountain, was for him
> No other world ; but this appeared his own

just long enough to make the loss an unforgetable thing. At last Caspar took up his parable and said :

"You know it is a wonderfully comfortable life one leads here in Germany, wandering from a *Bier-garten* lit with paper lanterns to a forest lit with stars, dissolving-view fashion. Can you think of anything pleasanter than the warm nights scented with syringa-bloom, when we have sat listening to the *Lorelei-lied* floating through the silence, and watching the fire-flies chasing each other among the branches above ? Did you ever catch a firefly in your fingers ? "

" Rather ! "

" And didn't you feel ashamed of yourself, and let it go again ? "

" As a matter of fact, I did ultimately let it go, because I could not find out how it lit itself and put itself out."

" But if dissection could have done it, you would have liked to know. Now there I differ from you. I fail to see what I can gain from finding out some instructive fact about ganglia or fibrillar epithelium. Let it remain in the air, out of reach, and keep it the untainted and mysteriously-beautiful thing that it is. Leave it alone ! "

" Well, hang it, man, I'm not going to touch it ! "

Pause, during which an examination of tickets took place through the window.

" I say, Charlie, do you remember, on

the occasion on which you first revealed yourself to me in London, we discoursed largely on the Value of Life " (in capitals), " where we all 'took a hand,' and came to the conclusion that the question was beyond discussion ? "

" Yes."

" Well, on reflecting over all the twaddle talked by myself and others on that occasion, and combining it with other ideas, I can't quite seize any particular purpose or use in the world at all. Of course when any of us says the world or universe, he means the world or universe so far as it concerns him and his intimate friends. Now what in the world is it all for, this seething mass of impotent wisdom, dominant stupidity and spite, wild desires, wilder delights, hopeless hopes, and hearts astray ? You are out in some still gloaming, with a wan primrose light in the horizon, with one great bright

E 2

star and two little ones above it, and you
are talking to a girl, and watching her eyes
begin to swim, and her head lean back to
look up into your face, and the sound of
the water, the smell of the firs, the voice
of the nightingale all say the same thing
to you ; and you understand it as well as
the language the stars speak together, till
you shiver as you almost overhear the passionless little jokes they make together at seeing
a man make such a fool of himself again,
for the billionth time, in the good old fashion.
Then you know that your faith will become
unfaith, and that all the picturesque, fervent,
and eternal love and truth and beauty which
you thought had entered your life are part
of a phantasmal gray joke, whose laughter
resounds through the hollows of hell. All
ideas of praise or blame are not in it here,
to use a convenient phrase. Give everyone
leave to seek his happiness frankly his own

way, and he straightway makes a ridiculous spectacle of himself, and either gets hung, labelled a hero by a leading article, or totally forgotten."

"And whistle o'er the lave o't!" replied Charlie, trying to adopt a cheerful and frivolous tone, though really terribly touched by his friend's wild talk.

For a week or two they walked from one village or small town to another in the Black Forest, which was what it always is in summer—a place for dreams, fairy tales, and moonlit wanderings, mental and otherwise. They came across occasional batches of students with knapsacks, who sang as they went along in the evening light, and were quite happy as long as they had beer, and could apply to a view, a sky, a variety of beer, or a country *Keller-mädel* impartially, their favourite epithets "*famos*!" and "*collossaal*!"

"The German student," observed Caspar, "is not a bad fellow, but he is a baby. Bearing that fact in mind, and taking care not to show that you find anything ridiculous in the things he thinks sacred and serious, such as a *Bier-comment* or a *Mensur*, you will find him a faithful friend and a jovial, if occasionally slightly besotted or wearisome companion. I think we grow old sooner in England ; in London of course we do. Then these fellows are always getting in love, and sending bouquets by *Dienstmänner* to some girl they once or twice have danced silently and solemnly with at the periodic ball. Then they become sombre, they rave (and occasionally weep a trifle) to all their friends, intimate and otherwise, under the seal of secrecy, over a *Liter-krug* of beer."

This sentiment Caspar delivered as they sat in the guest-room of an old inn, "Die Weisse Rose," with their elbows on an old wooden table, carved with the monogram of a student's corps, and with the nicknames of its various *Aktiver*, *Alte Herren* and *Conkneipanten*, in radiating lines.

"How long do you want to roam these woods and hills, spinning internal ghosts and seeing them?" asked Charlie.

"Why? Don't you enjoy it?"

"Of course I do, and am indebted to you more than I can ever repay for getting a benighted outsider like me into this part of the world pleasantly and safely."

"Nay, do not mock me, fellow-student."

"But I sometimes think you look as if you wanted to be back in England. You look tired, and bored, and seedy; and I think the Strand would be a good pick-you-up."

> "Siehest sterbe-blässlich aus,
> Sei getröst du bist zu Haus!

That's your idea?"

"Well, *Haus*, in that, is the only word that makes an intelligible appeal to me. You must not quote German to me which I shan't find in the text-book of Dr. Emil Otto."

"Don't you think these paths are better than the Strand? Here we have only our friends the fir-trees, and the old forest is like a great church, with starry-pointing spires; and in the deepest inmost shrine of its darkness, where the smell is sweeter than incense, and where all the noises of earth are far away and deadened, lives the spirit of the Schwarzwald, the elfin Commissioner of the Woods and Forests Department, placed there aforetime for those to find who could; and if a poor, sorrow-sick devil seeks her alone, he will find her by the one star far above her haunt, and she will take his tired head in her bosom and console him, as the whining infant that he is likes to be consoled."

There entered the room a young girl with roses to sell in a basket. She was pretty in a fair, outdoor, sunburnt style. Caspar looked at the roses, and at the girl. Then he spoke to her for a little while, and made her smile. She understood his German, but she did not understand the expression of the man who sat, leaning a dark wan face on his hand, and looking inquiringly up at her. She was a popular character, accustomed to the badinage of the travelling student, and was not very bashful; but here was something out of the common—a young man who made no attempt to clasp her waist, or to make foolish or coarse jests about her beauty. For once she felt instinctively both shy and pitiful without being quite able to give a reason for either.

"What will you let me have a rose for?" asked Caspar.

The two blue eyes looked into his brown
ones, and lost their shyness, keeping only
their pity; and the Schwarzwald *patois*
said :

"I will give you two roses—beauties—if
you will kiss me once."

And the bargain was made good, and
the girl escaped out of doors to think it
over.

"She is no *Juden-hetzer*," remarked
Caspar, with a quiet laugh. "She has not
been educated up to that pitch."

"This is all jolly interesting for me,
you know. Suppose you gave me one of
those ? "

Caspar threw him a rose, remarking :

"You weren't on in that scene, my
friend."

"I was not. I don't understand the evil
brogue you both talked in; but I understood the 'business.' I *must* learn German.

Somehow I don't believe old Otto and 'Charles has gone out riding with Mr. M.' to be exactly the quickest way. I think I shall spend my time speculating in roses."

"But (I speak as a fool) how about the Lilies in that connection?"

"Let us change the subject."

And a long silence ensued. The Swiss clock swung its pendulum on the wall, and the Frau Wirthin passed in and out at intervals, fetching a plate or a beer-mug. It was about nine o'clock in the evening by now, and nearly dark, as the "Weisse Rose" was plentifully overshadowed by trees.

"I am going out," suddenly remarked Caspar.

"What for?"

"Exercise."

"You have been walking all day."

"Well, I want to see the moon rise."

They went out among the motionless trees. A strange, pale haze was hanging over the farther reaches of the forest, luminous with the whole potency of the already risen full moon.

"This is almost better than I had hoped," said Caspar. "Don't you think it is one of the greatest and calmest pleasures in life to stand still, in the middle of a night like this, and drown your mind in the beauty of it, as in a pure and harmless intoxicant? This is the midmost shrine I spoke to you of, where lonely Nature shows her supremest sympathy with lonely men. Here the world is full of the still atmosphere of inexhaustible pity, instead of the merciless, glaring progress of daylight, the passionless scorn of the stars, or that inexorable roaring sea Shakespeare knew of. The bats seem too shy to fly; perhaps they are tired, like me. Oh, heaven and earth! Charlie, let this be my last night in Germany. Let us go away to-morrow morning to England, and I won't bore you any more with this drivel. We will hear a music-hall song; we will be funny and flippant, and pretend to rail on women; we will take cold Irish and soda, and flirt with barmaids; I will review bad novels, and you shall dress abscesses. You were right. I want to be at home again. I feel a great deal too amiable and compassionate to mankind. I'm sure that's a symptom of something seriously wrong with my mental health. But it's a transitory symptom, and ought to vanish in London."

"I think you had better come away. You are talking utter rot by the yard, and are quite different from what you generally are. I shan't know what to do with you if you become violent, you know."

"Well, suppose you go in and unpack our night-shirts."

" Very well.   Don't stray too far."

" No fear."

Charlie reluctantly left his friend, and walked slowly towards the inn.   At the door he turned round and looked behind him.   The form of Caspar was dimly discernible, leaning against a tree, around which he had wound one arm.   On this arm his head leaned back, and looked up into the sky.   Then Charlie went indoors.   Some short while after, Caspar strode in, grim, wild-haired, and haggard.

" Well, what have you been doing ? "

" Dreaming—the worst dream I ever had ; and I don't know when I shall wake."

Part the Fourth.

A LOST SHEEP OF THE HOUSE OF ISRAEL.

CHAPTER I.

Princes, and ye whom pleasure quickeneth,
   Heed well this rhyme before your pleasure tire;
For life is sweet, but after life is death:
   This is the end of every man's desire.

AND Mrs. Brandon shut the book, and leaned back in the low deep chair, with long eyes narrowing into a laugh. They were very fine eyes, with a feline softness about them, almost a caress, as they looked at the listener to the above verse. "Shall I go on?" she said.

Claudius Farringdon, pale as usual, the same neat semi-bald head, with black bilateral patch of hair above the forehead, the same iron-gray moustache, with long waxed spikes pointing symmetrically outwards, the same faded eyes, was sitting in his usual place in that study that looked toward the lawn where the sundial was. Claudius, speaking lazily and indistinctly, with a long cigar between his teeth, replied:

"No. It is very nice, and very cheering for an elderly man, but I think that will do for the present. Whenever you get the bit in your teeth as to what to read, you select something superfluously funereal. I don't know why."

"I thought it seasonable and appropriate."

"Thanks. I am afraid I can't recommend you as an agreeable companion to the average elderly gentleman. I don't mind, myself; in fact, it's rather interesting to watch the progress of one's own declining vigour. Have you sent that letter to George?"

"Yes."

"H'm! We will get that wedding over, and the two young fools—and the two old fools—out of the house as soon as possible. That letter ought to bring them."

"Yes."

"Why are you so motionless and sombre and subtle this afternoon—so mysteriously monosyllabic?"

"I didn't mean to be mysterious. I said yes, because I didn't know of anything more interesting to say."

"Do you know you are rather provoking? Of course you know it, though. You always do know your part well. Do you study expressions and tones in private, Jessie?"

"I know my part, as you say. I know you too, and that it is only by occasionally irritating you that one can keep you content. You have the palate of your—well, maturity, and it demands sharp sauces."

"You are still a very charming woman,

though one of Venetian supersubtlety, too. How old are you now?"

"Twenty-seven."

"By Jove—yes, so you are. It must be twelve years since I discovered you. You looked very nice then; but it was rather an unkempt, untutored niceness, you know, before I selected proper books and plays and habits for you. You always had a taste of your own for colour and costume, and have, I may remark, indulged it freely. But your accomplishments, and, perhaps, to some extent, your opinions, are my work. How is it you are not more inclined to desert me, and find some wider and more—er—profitable field for the display of your talents and attractions?"

"Gratitude, perhaps."

"You were always marked by the responsive tenderness of your emotions, weren't you? In fact, you like me with all the disinterested attachment of a young woman for an old man, and watch over me as a wild cat might watch her captor or her captive, with certain claws and teeth ready for either, should occasion demand."

"I mean now to watch you like either of the beings you talk about, until—well, until you don't require any more watching, if you want to know."

"And supposing I had rather go without that attention?"

"And told me to go? Gave me, in the delicate language of my childhood, the sack? Well, the result would be very simple. You would be alone. Your affable temper, your particularly attractive and philanthropic principles, your fluent tongue, and your numerous accomplishments, have at last brought you to the condition that you, Claudius, have, beyond me, not a friend in the world. I was fool enough, as a young girl, to do what many other foolish young girls probably did, I loved you. And with us that means something a little different from the pretty emotions of fair Saxons. When a woman of my race loves a man, she would cut her body in pieces for him, lie for him, steal or murder for him."

"Give up everything, except her dresses and her looking-glass, I daresay. You libel your interesting sex and nation, I hope."

"And when she finds afterwards that that man's love is a sham, that he bid for her as he would for a china saucer or an old book, don't you suppose that it makes some difference to her? Can't you understand how she loses most of her scruples, and her love of her fellow-creatures, as well as her self-respect?"

"But I still don't quite see the point of all this. You never talked like this before, though you do occasionally emit a rather sour remark. I thought, perhaps, you were going to pose for that style, imagining it to be attractive. If I'm such a very objectionable person, why don't you go away? If I'm ill, or want admiration, applause, love, amusement, cigars, or doctors, I can always get the best varieties and brands by paying for them."

"For a long time, Claudius Farringdon, I have noticed that you are drifting to death."

"What do you mean? Are you the family ghoul?"

"You are sliding down a slope steeper than you think. It is interesting, as you just now said, though you did not mean it, to watch your collapse, to see that elegant body and that brilliant brain changing slowly into a mass of useless and rather ugly matter, only fit to put into a leaden box, with a coat-of-arms and a label on it.

And nobody will be sorry. Not a soul. Your son's grief will be very temperate—a good deal discounted by the compensating fact of his inheritance; and as you never did anything noble in your life, you will be forgotten even sooner than those dead who really were noble."

"Thy most exquisite reason for this exhilarating prophecy?"

"I have watched when you did not notice it."

"Yes, I did. However, go on."

"You walk very oddly."

"No, I don't. Nobody sees it. I don't see it."

"Not the only thing you don't see. You asked me the other day why I had a green dress on. I did not think it worth while to argue about it, but I had no green dress on."

"Eh?" Claudius was now a little startled. 'Are you lying, or are you a devil come to torture me ? "

"Another thing, serious, too, for a good-looking man like you. The pupils of your eyes are different sizes."

"Don't suppose that matters much to me or anyone else. Anything else ? "

"You are losing your old art of tying a neckcloth neatly. And you walk very badly in the dark."

"But all this is, after all, very trivial, and hardly worth your tragic speech and pleasant allusion to the family vault."

"It is not trivial. I have read all about it."

"The devil you have ! "

"And know it all by heart. It was an accidental case of a man I saw in the street in London one day put it into my head, and I asked questions, and found references, and——"

"Well ? "

" He was walking oddly. I will not describe it. I read about celebrated cases.
They all began like you, and they all—all,
mind—died soon, in many unpleasant ways."

"Ha ! Well, if it be now, it will not be
to come. I may be all the villain you describe, but I am a gentleman, and death is
accepted by gentlemen quietly, as a necessary
evil. Have you any particular reason, beyond
the natural amiability of your disposition that
is to say, for wishing to convince yourself of
my approaching dissolution ? "

Jessica Rosenfeld—it is as well to give
her her name—got up from her lounging attitude, and knelt at Claudius's side, and kissed
the palms of both his hands fiercely and
repeatedly, saying :

" We women, and I of all women, are
mad, I think. I thought I hated you, but I
could love you more than ever, and die when

you died—together, like those people they drowned—if you would let me, darling. I want some one to love me, and make a child of me again. I never was a child, I think; and I never knew my mother; and you have tried to teach me to be bitter, and bright, and hard like yourself, and nearly succeeded. There may not be much more time; let us forget all the cruel things we have said, and all the clever books, and plays, and everything—let me have only real love for a little while, and I can go laughing through any hard life that change and time can bring. I feel like a lost child, with no home, no past, no country, no faith, no friends. I have nothing but you; and you will love me really, dear, won't you? Just say it once, and send me away if I bother you." And she laid her face on his velvet smoking-coat and sobbed nervously.

"Don't make yourself ridiculous and my

coat moist. If you had heard that kind of thing as often as I have you would know it doesn't fetch the intellectual stalls, though the gallery may wail. Get up and dry your eyes, and be sensible. Love is nonsense. I never loved anyone, and didn't usually believe it when anyone professed to love me. Much happier and quieter if you keep out of it."

The woman sprang upright, drawing quick breaths, as if about to say something violent. But she turned away slowly, and said in a low voice, as if to herself: "I don't care what becomes of me now."

Claudius stood up slowly, and mechanically lifted one hand to his moustache. He found it necessary to sit again.

"My God! and that fool of a doctor here said my pains were rheumatism—nothing more. I don't understand this."

What is mysterious is always more terrible than what is comprehensible. Claudius disliked these obscurely symptomatic changes —these occasional slips of hand or foot and twinges of pain—more than any severe commonplace suffering. The primitive nations of the earth either worshipped or execrated, in both cases feared, all phenomena they could not explain, and all *noumena* by which they explained them. The average modern is often not unlike his ancestor in this respect. The only difference is that he can explain a little, not much more. He does not perhaps burn witches, but he pays money to mediums. He does not often journey to consult the Delphic oracle, but he often is found deeply versed in Zadkiel's Almanac.

Claudius Farringdon would not probably have done any of these things; but he was distinctly alarmed now, and realised that before the irresistible, invisible, slow push from the hands of Death even gentlemen of ancient lineage, warlike ancestry, Epicurean education, and cultured taste must stagger and give in, and that not too gracefully.

"Tell me what else you know about this," he said. "I shall send for some specialist from town to-morrow."

"I don't know anything about any other disease, but I have learnt this one by heart. Stand still, with your feet together, and shut your eyes."

Claudius obeyed, rather puzzled. In about fifteen seconds he swayed backwards and fell with gradual acceleration into his chair in a heap.

Then he believed, and trembled.

"Don't leave me, Jessie, while I last," he said, this time perceiving the occasional indistinctness of his words.

She stood pale and still, looking down on him.

"Poor thing!" she said. "You are a coward, after all. Yes, I'll stay with you.

I'll put poison in your wine if you dare to drink it. Dare you?"

"We will see a London physician to-morrow."

"I will write about it. I want to go away to town myself for a few hours."

"Don't be long, How long does this sort of thing take, do you know?"

"I don't know. No one does. It varies. You have been building up this sepulchre for yourself all your life. And I mean to see it shut on you. Good-bye for the present." And she left the room.

Her next proceeding was to change her dress, put on her outdoor attire, and walk out at the front door. There, almost on the threshold, she encountered Alphonse the valet —a shaven, black-muzzled, ape-like Parisian, who had the general aspect of a well-to-do comedian. He touched his hat, saying: "The letter-bag, madame."

"Oh, let me see! Very well, Alphonse, I will take it to monsieur."

The valet delivered up his bag, touched his hat again, and disappeared, humming a little tune about the admirers and adventures of a person called Amanda, about whom it is sufficient to state that though it is not known how good she should have been, it is certain that she was no better. He also made a quaint grimace when he ascertained that he was unobserved save by a female servant, which childlike performance brought to his simple mind relief and satisfaction.

Madame took the letter-bag again into the study, where Claudius still sat motionless and thoughtful.

"Pick out the letters, please," he said; "tell me if any look interesting."

After casting aside circulars, prospectuses of benevolent societies, accounts rendered, cards for afternoon parties, etc., she selected a letter with a rather neat blue-and-white stamp in the corner.

"Here is one from your son, from Dresden. Shall I read it?"

"He is prompter than usual in replying. Yes, read it by all means."

"'Dresden, Saturday. Hotel Kaiserhof.'"

"That is one of his nice business-like habits to date a letter 'Saturday.'"

"I don't want him to have business-like habits. They would only delude him into thinking himself capable of competing financially with your astute compatriots, my dear. You don't like him, I know. However, read on."

"'Dear Governor,—Got yours this afternoon. Sorry to hear of your state. Will follow this letter home. Have reasons of my own for wishing to hurry wedding, which I daresay you won't mind taking place from the Manor House.'"

"And give Kimburls, etc., beds! Like his infernal impudence. Continue."

"'You, of course, will *congédier* (delicate word that, I take it) Mrs. Brandon, *pro tem.* Won't require more than a few days to turn us off.'"

"Fine prose style. Anything more?"

"'Will you "of course *congédier*" me?'"

"With this wedding taking place in my house, the prejudices of such society as would be represented there demand it; and as it will not cause me any very great or prolonged trouble, and may on the whole amuse me, the wedding will take place here, and you will amuse yourself in town for a few days, or anywhere else you please. Let us have the rest of the letter."

"'Talking of which, I don't know who Mrs. B. is, or where she comes from; but a fellow crossed our path this trip who sometimes reminded me of her appearance.'"

Mrs. Brandon pinched the paper rather hard, and read on :

" 'He was travelling as tutor, or something—I don't know—to young Deane, whose people live at Sokebridge, you know. He struck me as a howling cad, a member of the Hebrew persuasion, with most obnoxious opinions and a most impertinent manner of expressing them. When I saw him talking to Dick I felt inclined to kick him. He was evidently much struck with Dick, and pestered her with his attentions, which naturally made her uncomfortable.' "

" Is he sure it was Dick that was made to feel uncomfortable, I wonder ? " remarked Claudius.

" 'The fellow was rather good-looking in a way I don't admire, but awfully bad form. I believe some vague suggestion was heard that he should come to the wedding ; but that is one of the engagements I fancy

one had better forget. It would only upset
Dick and do nobody any good. Deane might
come; he is a neighbour and a gentleman.
The other fellow's name is Caspar Rosenfeld.
We shall arrive, bar accident, about twelve
hours after this—Kimburls, Miss Menteith,
Dick, and self.—Your affectionate son,

"' GEORGE MALCOLM FARRINGDON.'"

"So I have to take them all whether I
like it or not. I say, Jessie, my affectionate
son doesn't know quite what an interesting
letter that is to you, eh?"

"No; nor do you. But he will. Look
here; of course it is understood that I go
away during this wedding. If you don't
mind I'll go this evening, as I don't want
to see any of these people."

"Go when you like. I am sorry, but
go."

CHAPTER II.

The sea hath its pearls,
The heaven hath its stars.

AT six o'clock on a still August afternoon,
shortly after that other evening spent in
the moonlit Black Forest, Caspar stood in
the bows of the large steamer *Lady Tyler*,
watching the gradual advance of that vessel
between the multitudinous wide mud-banks
which flank the seaward road from quaint,
parti-coloured, old Rotterdam, while the long
sun-path over the ripples became slowly less
dazzling and deeper coloured straight ahead
of the ship.

Charlie was below, satisfying a hearty

appetite which had not been legitimately
appeased through some twenty-eight slow
hours of dusty, hot, second-class German and
Dutch railway-travelling.

Caspar paid no attention to the confused
crowd of passengers, luggage, horses, oozing
fruit hampers, and barrels of butterine, which
the Dutch dock labourers had piled miscel-
laneously about the deck, or to the anxious
speculations of bystanders as to the proba-
bilities of a pacific passage. One nervous
old gentleman ventured to ask his opinion
on that subject, saying, "Do you think there
is any danger in these vessels, sir?" Caspar
gently replied, "I don't think there is any
hope of *this* one sinking," and was spared
further inquiries.

And then he leaned alone on the bulwark,
with one arm around an iron stanchion,
listening to the rush of water driven in lateral
wrinkles by the passage of the vessel. And

the hollow murmurous swirl of the sea sang
to him in a thousand different variations of
tune—one song, one long chorus of pity
and dreamy desolation. The water was
white, glittering, still, and hazy away right
and left and ahead among the low, green,
misty mud-islands, until it reached a line of
gray-purple waves and white foam-streaks
which marked the threshold of the open sea.
Small dark-sailed craft were passed by the
steamer, with the full light of the descending
sun throwing their warm madder or carmine
canvas into strong relief against the wan
waste of water. Or perhaps they appeared
ahead as dark sharply-defined obstructions
to the sunlight.

And then the foamy frontier of the
Channel became faintly tinged with pink,
while the sky became hazy, coppery-red,
merging into deep yellow, and then undefined
warm transparent gray under the cloudless

blue. The ship steamed sedately on, giving
a slight roll as the groundswell made itself
manifest, while the western haze became
warmer in colour, the sun sank lower, and
the waters sang louder. And Caspar Rosenfeld, with his coat wrapped round him,
catching occasional dashes of cold salt spray
across his eyes and lips from the little waves
that broke and splashed, shaped the sea-
chime gradually almost against his will into
some sort of words. And these were of
them :

> For in your eyes I think I once have seen
>   A light like love, that meant the world to me,
> God help me! dreaming of what might have been:
>   God help you! for it was too good to be.

"Why in the world did I ever go to
Schlangenberg, I wonder? And now that
I have found it to be the best resting-place
of all my restless life, I wonder if I ever
can go back to it again? I wonder what

things such a fellow as I am is likely to
enjoy for the remainder of his period of crawling between earth and heaven ? And when
my face has become 'the map of days out-
worn,' and my hand has been played, my stake
lost, my last glass emptied, my last quarter's
rent due to the Fates paid, what shall it profit
me to remember that I have surrendered
and lost the best thing earth ever offered
me ? What hinders me from now resting
under, instead of steaming over, this glanc-
ing green and purple sea ? I suppose because I like still to dream of the most
beautiful valley in the world, containing the
town where I lost you for ever—you fair
pure little girl, whose face follows me, and
looks at me out of foam-framed mirrors,
coloured like a lily lit with the Abend-roth.
That is behind me now, and there is only
left what is before me—the vague shimmering sea, without visible limits, with a fierce

red sun sinking away from sight, and mark-
ing our roadway in fire, till we reach some
later darkness where there are no stars."

"It is very cold," observes Charlie, at
that instant appearing, pipe-smoking, ulster-
clad.

"It is a nipping and an eager air."

"Why the devil then don't you come
below? There's some tea and beer going."

"I don't want any tea, or even beer. I
want to look at this sea and sky, and see
the last of the 'Low Countries,' as our dear
writers of an earlier day call them."

"You want to observe the revolutions of
the paddles?"

"Yes."

"What do we do when we get to the
other side?"

"Go to Liverpool Street, where we arrive
at some comfortless hour of the morning.
Then we drive to Barnard's Inn, wash, and

breakfast, after which you may do what you like."

" I must go home, I think."

" By all means.   Give my compliments to your people."

" That wedding of Farringdon's is expected to come off there soon.   They are on their way back, if they haven't arrived, I'm informed."

" Give them my hearty congratulations."

" All right."

And the steamer sped on in chase of the vanishing sun.

When there was no longer any daylight, only a coppery-gray ghostly similitude of a sunset sky reflected in the east, behold, there appeared dimly through this cloud-curtain the golden round moon, which had transformed the Black Forest into a scene from an elfin tale, by the aid of a few trifling ounces of aqueous vapour, a day or two before. It now changed the colour of the sea from purple shades and pink lights to pale shimmering gray. The water-surface began to lose its level appearance, and to resemble in places great sloping slabs of glistening oily matter, among which phosphorescent flashes glanced from time to time, like lightning between colliding clouds. And the moon's exaggerated circle became smaller, paler, and brighter, and the whole sea flickered. The deck and boats of the steamer gleamed white, while Caspar's figure and the neighbouring ropes and fittings looked like brown etchings. And their shadows swayed to and fro across the rocking moonlit deck.

"Did it ever occur to you," observed he suddenly, "to think how you would like to die?"

"The way that hurt least."

"In bed, composing your last words, or your last words but one; in fact, taking your farewell benefit among an admiring and weeping audience of relatives and friends and remote descendants, with a special reporter in a corner taking memoranda for the last pages of your biography? Or on the tented field, waving a fragmentary blade, and casually observing 'Victory!' to any bystander who might be at leisure to listen—aforesaid verbatim reporter, for example; you always find him lurking near heroes' death-scenes? Or swirling round and round in the wash of the Maëlstrom? Or going up in a fragmentary condition, with cinders and lava and whatever is left of the late Enceladus, towards the heavens, and descending like a rocket-stick?"

Charlie suggested prussic acid as the most rapid and painless method.

" But that involves the notion of suicide, as well as the consequent notion of a stuffy tavern, and nervous jurymen 'view-

ing' you hurriedly (*vide* Dickens), and returning a complicated verdict in dubious
grammar, in which the visitation of Heaven,
temporary insanity, censure of a chemist,
and beetle-poison would be artlessly mixed
together, followed by a paragraph in the
afternoon papers. All of which painfully
vulgar, and very poor from an artistic point
of view."

"Would you mind explaining the tendency of all this discourse?"

"I don't know that it has any particular
tendency. I was throwing out observations
at large, on an interesting topic. I think
the moonlight is going to my head a little.
I should like to take the stars and treat them
as a fount of fiery gold type, and set them
up into sentences, in capital letters, with
planets for stops and comets for commas, so
that I could transmit messages from myself
to the limitless universe. I would print

such a song as the spheres would chime to, and the meteors dance, on the brows of the darkness of space, like fireflies in the black wild-woven hair of a bacchanal. And I would sign my name with a flourish at the bottom, with that celebrated fir-tree dipped into Etna."

"And what would the song be?"

"It ought to be in that language that is so rich and beautiful that all philologists are deaf and blind to it. It would tell how the sea is made up of all the tears of all time from sorrow-laden men and women, who lost all that made their lives beautiful and happy; and from all the poor children who are lost and beaten and starved and mis-understood; of those old men whom their children think bores when they become in-firm and childish, and laugh at and neglect, and will not listen to their old stories, though the same old hands that now spill

the soup from the spoon have once made them
toys; and all the girls who have loved men
who grew tired of them, who lied to them
or bullied and struck them; all the desolate
destitute who sell their bodies at last; all
the great sleepless, enslaved, and oppressed
of the whole world, from the east to the
west; all who have lost their hearts' delight
come and tell their grief under the still
summer starlight to the sea, and one or two
of them find the sea sing them such a soothing song that, listening to it, they follow and
fall asleep for ever.

"And all the great men of old time, who
hold out to us the hand of pity, and send
us the voice of tears in laughter across the
centuries, have sent the echo of their dead
immortal voices out to the listening world,
in the eternally-varying monotony of the
music of the sea. Here in the German
Ocean, not far from Holland, you hear in

the *Rausch* of the waves sometimes the infinite sympathy and serene majesty of Shakespeare saying :

> Take all my loves, my love ; yea, take them all :
> What hast thou then more than thou hadst before ?

And from below come faintly up the peals of bells of buried cities, where people once lived and loved and sorrowed, who are at peace for ever. And at last comes the answer to all my riddles of time and life, in the mocking retort of the sea-nymphs, who say :

> It is night in your brain,
> And the lightnings of madness flash through it ;
> And for very sorrow you are a very driveller."

"Poor old chap !" observed Charlie, staggering as the swell increased. "Hadn't you better go below and sleep ?"

"It is a relief to me to have got all that interesting gush of bile off my system, to use a graceful metaphor. I didn't know you were attending or listening. Why didn't you put in derisive cheers? Somebody ought to stop me when I come out with the utterances of irresponsible frivolity."

"I thought you mightn't be safe to interfere with. I thought perhaps you didn't feel well."

"Nor do I; but it is the sea-sickness of that weary bark one has heard of that I suffer from, not the ordinary basin variety."

"What do you mean?"

"There's a reference in it; you can look it up and find it in a dictionary of quotations if .you can. You had better go to bed, or turn in, or whatever these nautical people call it."

"What do you mean to do all night?"

"Stay here. Nights like these are too good to lose."

And when the cold yellow blaze of dawn

displayed the English coast, Caspar was walking the deck, when Charlie ascended, shivering in his ulster, to look around him.

"Well, what of the night?"

"On reflection, I believe my talk to have been the veriest rot; wasn't it? I hope you didn't pay any attention to it?"

"Not the least."

"Then let us breakfast before we have to go ashore. The night and the sea have separated us from Germany now; we are in British waters, and the dreaming time is over. We will read sporting papers and go to the Gaiety bar; we will drink the porter-beer, sell wives in Smithfield, and box. Steward! what will you give me per pound avoirdupois of lesser German coinage?"

"I say," observed Charlie after a pause, while the shivering, insufficiently-washed, tired, and sleepy passengers were assembling on deck as the steamer got alongside its

H 2

pier—" I say, what a holy show that fellow is ! You should have seen his preparations for sleep and sickness down below. He tied an awful handkerchief, meant to be white, round that cap, and when the ship lurched he read a small book backwards. I couldn't help noticing him. I found the book when he had gone up for a minute or two to be sick, or look at the view, or something ; it was Hebrew, as well as dirty, and had 'Julius Bloemendaal, 29, Castle Street,' inside."

Caspar looked at the man.

"A Dutch Jew ; not prettier than the average. They don't show to advantage at sea. They will sometimes persist in wearing those cloth caps and long coats. Are you certain that was the address ? "

" Quite. Why ? "

" Oh, I don't know who the house belongs to now, of course. I was mistaken. It doesn't signify."

But Caspar eyed this person keenly as they ascended the greasy gangway, bag in hand, ticket in mouth. The traveller did not notice Caspar at all, and went into the Custom House to wait for some parcels. Caspar and Charlie got into the train, and they saw the stranger, who was a caricature of the ordinary dingy and sea-sick Dutchman, no more.

In the foggy orange-red light of a London morning, at that cheerful resort called the Great Eastern Terminus, E.C., with the lurid colouring of the atmosphere on their faces and hands, Charlie and Caspar entered a cab and started for Barnard's Inn.

"Awfully glad I am to get back to the dear, squalid, jolly old town again!" exclaims the former.

"So am I."

"Still we had about as good a time as they make it, I think."

"Very likely. Now don't begin that sort of thing immediately you get your feet in a hansom, or I shall turn rusty. I don't want to talk about Germany just at present. Let's get a daily paper, and discuss police cases and inquests and new burlesques."

And this because there rang yet in his brain, faintly borne over the past moonlit sea, the far-off echo from the forest-clad Schlangenthal :

God help you ! dreaming of what might have been ;
God help you ! for it was too good to be,

which he knew the heart of his life would hear for ever.

CHAPTER III.

What did I feel that night? You are curious.
How should I tell?

IN the great art-gallery of Dresden, George
Farringdon and Dick Menteith were wandering, a little ahead of Kimburls and Miss
Menteith; and they were all supposed to be
looking at the pictures. The laird, indeed,
was rashly critical, and used the expression
"bradth" a good deal, until his daughter
asked him what he meant, on which he
sought for new expressions, and wallowed in-
tellectually in polysyllabic definitions, until
she was sorry she spoke. He was particularly attracted by cattle pictures. It is
difficult to say why. He was not at all an

authority on agricultural matters; but it probably came within his theory of feudal chieftainship to imagine himself endowed, if not with vast herds, at any rate with a vast power of criticising other people's. George, who had been there before, and ascertained which works it was right to admire, guided them straightway to The Madonna. Miss Menteith senior disapproved of pictures of this description, because they savoured of a lady late of Babylon, "fond of flirtation and dressing in red," as the dear late poet of "Ingoldsby" hath it. Kimburls saw that this was not quite the same as the dozen and odd other Madonnas he had seen already, here and elsewhere, and to his credit be it said that he ventured no remarks upon it. George was inclined to be rapturous in a low voice, with the language of the subject picked up at Oxford. Poor Dick, who could not understand why she felt nervous and ill at ease, looked up at that face with some vague and inarticulate

> O neige
> Du Schmerzenreiche!

written in her dumb eyes. She had not read "Faust;" she did not know enough German. She was only a little Scotch girl of eighteen, who did not cast about for heroic or pathetic quotations in which to express feelings too foreign for her own vocabulary.

She felt that she ought to be very happy. She was walking about in a pleasant place, with the man she was going to marry, whom she liked, and had liked for years, and she was going to please her parents, and gain a certain position (and probably a "stake"), by so doing. And yet she almost caught the faint echo of the laugh of that "phantasmal gray joke" Caspar spoke of.

The roof and the air seemed heavy, the beautiful far-off country along the Elbe seemed strangely sad, and she felt, above all, anxious to get back to England. And just once— it may have been from a faint fantastic resemblance in some Velasquez portrait, and it may have been the irresistible self-assertion of nature breaking through the dutiful and peaceful monotony of habit— the personal image of Caspar Rosenfeld came into her mind ; and if she had been left alone to think herself out under the eyes of the apotheosised Mother, the chances are strongly in favour of the occurrence of a revolution in her ideas on certain matters. But she was interrupted by George, who, keenly watching her face, said: "I think you have had enough of this place, Dick, and the laird looks as bored as he can be ; and between ourselves I am getting rather in the like state. Let us go."

" Very well."

" I say, I know now what you are languishing after—some of those ices at the Café Français. We will go round there. Kimburls and your aunt are not above such comforts, I know. And when a girl has your pathetic expression, Dick, one may generally safely put it down to hunger." George was an observer of human character, female and otherwise, you see, and it pleased him to give expression to his experiences in keen phrases.

" I think I am rather tired, George," Dick replied. " Yes, I daresay you may be right. I have an unsatisfied desire for ices."

" Oh, I'm away, Jeanie ! " remarked Kimburls. "My head is full of four centuries of fine arts wambling together."

And they followed George to a café.

Dick Menteith had been discovering slowly, in the course of some weeks past, that her relations' minds and ideas did not expand in the direct ratio of the demand made on them by novel, artistic, or naturally beautiful surroundings.   In fact, they thought and talked much as they usually did when at their residence in the immediate neighbourhood of Glasgow, hankered after their periodical home newspaper, and displayed undeniable and impenetrable opacity to the influences of environment, which keenly and deeply penetrated Dick.   Even with George she was not at all times perfectly satisfied.   She was the victim of mental distress, consisting of a vague anxiety founded on physical weakness, excitement, and fatigue, and other and obscurer causes.

She did not sleep very well, and had strange and not always pleasant dreams.

Miss Menteith noticed that her niece seemed pale and out of sorts, and mentioned the fact to Kimburls, who recommended a "rhubarb peel." George slept profoundly, and digested moderately well. He had scraped acquaintance with one or two roving young Englishmen who imagined themselves to be "reading," and, through ignorance of the language and habits of the place, made billiards and the consumption of mixed drinks their chief amusement.

And Dick had no one but him to whom to reveal her ideas confidentially. And he did his best to understand, and to criticise from the omniscient Farringdonian and Oxonian standpoint, whether he understood or not. Dick never got as far as to speculate whether it was her bounden duty or not to marry this young man. She had a strangely feverish desire to accelerate their marriage, and was more anxious thereanent than she dared say.

She was afraid of something, she knew not what. At last the slow-moving Kimburls made her see a doctor; an old Englishman, with a gray beard and gold spectacles, who, after tapping her chest and back, and asking questions, said to her father:

"There's nothing the matter with her except a little nervousness and fatigue; would be hysteria in a weaker girl. Been brought up in the country on porridge and milk, I hope?"

"Lairgely."

"I'll give her a little tonic. She has nothing to be anxious about, I take it?"

"Not she! She will be marryin' when we're away again to England, and has her man with her."

"Happy days, happy days! Ha, couldn't do better. Thank you. Yes. Good-morning."

And all science revealed to Dick was that she was in a fair way to salvation, if she married George Farringdon.

And the dicta of science coincided with

those of her relations, and of what she supposed to be her conscience.

And one last afternoon, as she and her
lover were walking in the evening alongside
the Elbe, looking onwards to the great red
fringe of western clouds over the bridge join-
ing the Altstadt . and Neustadt, Dick found
herself in a kind of day-dream, relating to
a conversation on the terrace of the old
Schlangenberg Schloss at a similar time of
day, earlier in the summer ; on which occasion
it had been prophesied that she would like
Dresden less than the Schlangenthal. And
she was a little tremulous when she said
to George : " Do you think that is as beautiful
as Schlangenberg was ? "

"That what is as beautiful ? Oh, the
scene ! Well, on the whole, yes. I would
as soon be in the one place as the other,
with you, little girl, to make remarks on
and to add to the beauty of scenes ; but I

think this is a more civilised place than Schlangenberg. You meet better people, and can get better things. That Kron-Prinz *table d'hôte* was disgraceful. A college-hall couldn't have done it worse."

This was the evening on which Caspar and Charlie were supping on black bread, cheese and eggs, and beer, in the guest-room of the inn of " The White Rose," in the pine-forest

Made sad by dew, and wind, and tree-barred moon.

" I think we will all be glad to return to England—don't you ? "

" I do. And that reminds me that I have had a letter from the governor to-day I wanted to mention to you. He doesn't often write, and when he does he generally has a pretty definite reason. He says—well, I'll give you some extracts : ' If you want me to be present in an efficient state at your

wedding, I strongly recommend you to accelerate it, as I have found my health deterio-
rating lately. I have curious sudden sharp
pains about my body, and the doctor, who
tries to look as if he knew all about it,
suggests an approaching · attack of gout or
rheumatism. I asked him if that would
account for my occasional partial deafness,
and he said I must take care of myself. I told him I had spent all my life
in taking care of no one else. I think
people of my habits and tastes ought to
have an omniscient doctor as a kind of
permanent body servant, to tell them exactly
what to eat and drink, and how long to
sleep, etc., so as to get the utmost value
out of life, and balance dissipation and
recuperation with scientific accuracy. The
fact is, I'm getting old, I believe, and may
expect legitimate promotion to the upper or
lower house before many years. It is, per-

haps, just as well, as I have done and read nearly all the amusing things that a man of intelligence and taste can. Besides, my exit will be convenient for you at the approaching crisis of your existence."

" Now, what puzzles me about this," continued George, " is that it is not in his handwriting, and, lazy as he is, I never knew him dictate a letter before. That is very curious. But I do suggest that we go home as soon as we can, and get this wedding business settled and done with. What do you say ? "

" George, will it make you really happy if I marry you, do you think ? "

" What do you mean ? Why do you talk like that ? "

" I mean, would it be a very terrible thing if you were to lose me ? "

" Lose you ! If you married anyone else I think I should shoot him, if you want to know."

Dick sighed.

"Very well, dear."

"Don't let us ever argue about that any more, if you don't mind."

"I never will again. And, George, let us go home now; I want to rest and think."

As Dick walked back with him along the riverside late in the saffron twilight, she made up her mind that she must marry George Farringdon as soon as possible. It was now her evident duty as it had been her hoped-for privilege. And now, for the first time, did she experience that slight waning of attraction which occurs in a hoped-for privilege which has become an evident duty—that faint trace of repulsiveness inherent in such actions as seem obvious moral necessities, where liberty of action becomes subordinate to what is called the dictate of conscience. She lay thinking on her bed that evening, watching the gentle

onset of darkness, and listening to the music
and murmur of the town.   Music always
mixes with the evening of a people set free
from their work in a German town.

And she dreamed awake of the days gone
by in detached scraps of scenes : of ballads
first heard on the nurse's knees by the fire-
light, which wakened her first interest in
those strange passionate tragedies in unforgetable verse which illustrate the lurid book
of Scotch history ; of sesquipedal soporific
sermons from Mr. Toumharns the Free and
far from " stickit " minister, which she, a
weary little person in a short frock, had been
constrained to "sit under"; of paddling in
streams with cut feet; of personated scenes
from the mystic and magical panorama displayed by the author of " Waverley ;" of red-
gowned students hurrying through dark foggy
streets ; of fiery song-tunes provoked in the
autumn gloaming from the old piano about

the Young Chevalier, General Sir John Cope, or the man for whose sake the bells rang backward and the drums beat as he rode to the West Port; of a comely young Englishman, whose presence made a refreshing variation in the circle of legal toddy-consumers and dry anecdote-retailers, whom Kimburls delighted to honour and was wont to entertain; of New Year nights spent merrily, when the laird forgot his dignity in the unbridled and athletic license of the Houlachan; and lastly, of clear summer evenings of a new and unsurpassed beauty, in which she had talked a few short sentences with the strange pale man with the pleasant voice, whom she never would see, in all probability, again. And the stars came out, the people wandered and murmured below, and the distant music floated in through the open window. Such retrospective visions, they say, come to drowning men.

CHAPTER IV.

JESSICA STUDIES THE ROLE OF ATE.

WHEN Jessica Rosenfeld left Sokebridge Manor, it was to the railway station that she walked with a rapid but graceful gait, and face reminding one of those beautiful sudden summer storms, when the sky has become gray and purple, the buildings livid, and the wind has begun to lift the dust and shake the leaves. She did not display any great unevenness of manner or uneasiness of mind; but a passer-by would certainly have looked at her, and almost as certainly have remarked first, "Pretty woman, that!"

second, "Looks sulky, rather; wonder what she's after?" What she was after at present was a train to London Bridge, which she caught. And she lay back languid but stern, with those splendid Semitic eyes darkling under a pair of menacing level brows, waking conjecture in the minds of her fellow first-class passengers. Hers was a curious face. The nose was straight in repose, but became slightly aquiline by a peculiar, and to many people pleasing, muscular action when she smiled. She did not smile very often, but when she did, the likeness to her brother became almost suddenly manifest.

Her meditations, as she sat in that carriage opposite a colonial bishop and his lady, were strange—principally on her spoilt life, her fervent and foolish youth, her weary and hopeless womanhood, and her last passionate breakdown, in which the hot floods of insuperable natural passion had at last

rent their thin coating of superinduced con-
ventional ice, to be again petrified by the
cold bitterness of ungrateful laughter. This
time, indeed, the love once possible was
"drowned, frozen, dead for ever;" and a
certain grim and growing determination succeeded to it that the laughter should not
always lie on one side. And that unhappy
letter of George Farringdon's had suggested
to her the vision of a catastrophe to that
young man and his family, as yet dim and
misshapen, in which she would one day
appear as the triumphant avenger of that
long-seeming life of hers, where all that
was pure and happy and womanly in the
good sense had been lost and spoilt, and
mocked to death, in which she would see
herself laughing amid the desolation and
ruin of the last of the Farringdon family.
And the colonial bishop opposite saw her
soundless laugh, and did not know whether

to feel admiration for her beauty or alarm
for her sanity most.

At London Bridge she alighted, called a
cab, and drove along King William Street
and Fenchurch Street to Aldgate. At the
corner of Leadenhall Street she dismissed
the cab, and walked on eastward to Duke
Street, up which she turned, ultimately
arriving at a house on one side of Castle
Street, Bevis Marks. A private house apparently, as no name or advertisement of any
kind appeared externally visible. A dingy,
smudged brick, early eighteenth-century
house, with a doorway and front all leaning
a little backwards. It had been, no doubt,
built upright originally, and had settled down
into its most comfortable position and stuck
to it. Though not inviting, or precisely
what might be called clean-looking, it suggested nothing disreputable. The windows
on the ground-floor revealed nothing, for

their blinds were down, and no light was apparent behind them. A street-lamp shed its light on the small, thick, shining brass figures of the number twenty-nine on the door, and the much newer black knocker below. It was now evening, in fact, rather late in the evening, and most of the shops in the neighbourhood were shut, except in not far distant Whitechapel, and the streets were pretty lively when Jessica knocked at the door. Nobody's attention seemed to be attracted by this performance, except that of the passers, mostly juvenile, who stared and made not very *sotto voce* remarks about her dress and appearance. Those level brows lowered again, and a further and more energetic application of the iron knocker to its anvil brought out a man—a dingy man, who looked like a true portion of the furniture of such a house. An acute inquiring face, with a short grizzly red beard, a long grizzly red hanging lock brushed forward over the upper flap, let us call it, of each ear, a rather beak-like nose, small rather angry-coloured eyes, surmounted by a soft black cloth cap with a peak, from under which reddish curls oozed behind; round his neck a discoloured red object, misnamed comforter, tightly knotted, formed a very characteristic colour-discord with his hair. His body was clothed in a long dark coat belted at the waist—of a taller man, once—and his legs, so far as they were visible, in wrinkled high boots, very aged, very ill-fitting, and tending upwards at the toes. Evidently a Jew; apparently a Dutch one.

"Vat you want?" He stood with the door-handle in his hand.

"Is Mr. Nathan Rosenfeld in?"

"You want to see eem?"

"I do."

"Vill you gif your name?"

"Jessica Rosenfeld."

"Ah, com in! You can see eem. Ee is eengeslapen."

"Gone to bed?"

"No. Groot stool—armchair. Com in late from te West. 'Ere is te room. 'Ere is Nathan Rosenfeld."

"Thanks. And who are you?"

"I am Julius Bloemendaal of Rotterdam, one of te people, and serfant or clerk, as you like, to Nathan Rosenfeld. Ee trost me vit——"

"With what?"

"Vit noting. Nathan Rosenfeld is a beautiful man, a groot man, a goot man."

"Thank you. Good-night."

Julius Bloemendaal of Rotterdam withdrew.

Jessica stood in a small back room, simply furnished with an old leathern chair, a table, a pewter inkstand, and a safe. An old man

was in the armchair asleep, with his mouth
open. A copy of the Old Testament Scriptures,
in their original tongue, was on the table,
a steel pen and some blue ink were in the
inkstand, and what was in the safe the owner
of it best knew. The said owner looked at
times venerable and rabbinical; but this was
not one of the times, as his head hung on one
side, with a gray beard pressed up crookedly
against his shoulder, a black skull-cap having
fallen on to the floor, where it lay in- and
unpleasant side uppermost; and all his limbs
had the peculiar Guy-Fawkes helplessness of
appearance peculiar to aged limbs when their
owner sleeps in a chair. A paraffin lamp
burned low on the mantelshelf, and its
presence was distinctly appreciable in the
room, apart from any little light it gave.

The old man was dressed respectably, but
shabbily, in black. Perhaps the blackest part
of the costume was the linen, as the cloth was

nearly white in the places most subject to
friction.   The head was as venerable as bald-
ness could make it, and the face curiously
apostolic—meanly apostolic.   I do not know
if Judas can be legitimately called an apostle.
But he was like Nathan Rosenfeld, I know.

Old Rosenfeld's occupations were various.

He was Marsden & Co., of Craven's Court,
W., in his elegantly got-up circulars, inform-
ing the youth of our Universities and Military
Academies of his willingness and ability to
advance ready money to any amount at
moderate interest. To impecunious young men
and maidens seeking situations as secretaries,
governesses, actresses, etc., he was an Educa-
tional and Dramatic Agency, on a brass plate
curving round a door-post in a street off the
Strand.   Here, young men with very elegant
manners and ready-made clothes kept large
metal-clasped books.   And in the books were
the names written of such as had had (and

usually lost) faith in the agency, and worshipped the golden mirage of hope which it
set up. And the guinea fees of them were
gathered together, and the books were opened
quarterly, and the commissions thereof divided
among the subordinates, in lieu of wages—a
plan which made them singularly apt at their
work of encouragement, urbanity, and inven-
tive procrastination.

To ambitious but obscure authors he was
the Society for the Introduction of Amateurs
to the Public, and "ran" a magazine in connection with it, where the Great Obscure paid
handsomely for the insertion of their valuable
contributions and a copy of the magazine containing them, which they showed joyously
and unsuspectingly to their surprised friends
as evidence that they were making a name in
literature in the distant metropolis.

He visited these various offices in rotation,
and was fully acquainted with the working

of them all, though he scarcely ever was
visible to a visitor. If he was seen he assumed
the air and dignity of a crossing-sweeper or
accidental charman, and disappeared. No one
suspected him of being the "guv'nor," as he
was styled by his reverent subordinates. The
wholesale and export clothing department had
been given up long ago for more fashionable
and lucrative speculations, such as the above ;
but he continued to reside in the house in
which he had originated the former business
in London. It was his own, and it was quite
good enough for him. Not having any particular tastes, he did not squander his money
in gratifying them. The pet amusement of
his leisure hours was the compilation and
correction of accounts kept, for reasons known
to himself, in Hebrew. He was not an exceptional monster, he was not a Barabas of
Malta ; but he was a rather ingenious man,
who knew the wants of his erring fellow-

creatures, and would consent to gratify them for a due recompense. And it appeared in his experience that, as a rule, the primary form of want, of gratification, and of recompense consisted of money. As long as they paid for it, it was immaterial to him how they used it, or even whether they ever indeed got it or not. And this elder was the father of Caspar and Jessica Rosenfeld. The latter woke him up by a well-placed prod with the point of her umbrella. He started and stared with the imbecile gravity of a recently-awakened man. He recognised his daughter with some surprise.

"Oh, you have come, have you? Take the chair, sit down, and tell me your news." And he replaced the skull cap on his head, reassuming with it the venerable appearance, turned up the lamp, and continued :

"I thought I was never going to see you again."

"I did not come for the pleasure of your society."

"Ho, ho! She didn't come for the pleasure of my society! And what did she come for? To visit the poor, to see how they live, in their daily plodding industry, their humble East-end homes? And is she going to leave me a tract? Or does she want her poor old father's hard-earned money to buy her dresses, eh?"

"Don't be a fool, Nathan Rosenfeld, and listen to me. My lord and master is going to die."

"Of course he is. So am I some day."

"But he is going to die soon. And his son will reign in his stead."

"Don't she look beautiful," muttered the old man, "with those clothes and that face, in this poor old room! And to think that all that is my work—my work! And she is ungrateful, and says, Don't be a fool!"

"And I say it again. It is of no use to talk like that to me. We know each other pretty well by this time. I want to talk business."

"Yes?" And Nathan became grave and eager. "Does the great Herr want money?"

"Claudius Farringdon? No. He never spent a penny over his income, and wasted nothing in charity. But his son is, as far as I know him, a fool, and will marry another, I believe, soon, and *they* will want it. Not yet. Later. Now listen. The son has not, and I think will not, have any idea as to who or what I am beyond what he sees. And if I induce him to spend money—he doesn't like me, you know, because I always snub him; but he shall, if I like—and if I recommend him to Marsden & Co.?"

"Mustn't recommend him to them. Nasty blood-sucking money-lenders. Bad lot!"

"Yes, I know they are. And you can speak with authority. I daresay you will expose them some day."

"Ho, ho! Yes. That is a good one. Expose them! Yes. Go on."

"Question is, will Marsden & Co. deal with him in their usual way?"

"I should not think they would consent to make any alterations in their usual terms, without good cause is shown. What do you want them to do?"

"Behave as usual."

"Aha! What for, now?"

"That is my business. My aims, and those of—well, Marsden & Co., if you like to keep up that little fiction, happen so far to coincide. You make your profit, and I," she added in a low voice, "make mine."

"How can you do this?"

"That is also my business."

"And supposing I refuse?"

"Then I should say you were a greater fool than I ever took you for. I might even threaten to expose Marsden and all the agencies—put you, your address in Castle Street, and your personal appearance and interesting biography, in a society paper, for example."

"Don't send the article to one of the papers I own, then." ("Had her there!" he reflected, with a pleased smile.)

"Which are they?"

"That is my business. All of them, perhaps."

"Well?"

"Is there no fraud? no law-breaking?"

"You always have such a respect for the law. No. Safe as any other of your transactions, any two of which would, I should think, put you in gaol for life, if you got your rights."

"Is this filial? is this affection? is this gratitude? I ask?"

"Don't talk to me about gratitude. You know how much of that is due from me better than most people."

"Well, but it is this, you know. I do not like making promises in the dark. I generally keep my promises; but I want to know the conditions first."

"How you do worry about nothing! I make you a very simple proposition, and, from your point of view, a very attractive one, and you argue and make scruples and pretences and difficulties as much as if I had come to borrow money of you. I might never have told you anything about my plan if I had liked to work things my own way."

"And why did you?"

"Because I thought it would make things simpler if you and I entered into a partnership of a purely business nature."

"Oh! And what commission or profit might you want?"

" None that I shall not have without your help."

" No money ? "

" Claudius will provide for me, I believe."

" You believe. Where will he find the money then ?

" Where he generally does find it, I suppose."

" And where do you think that is ? "

" I don't know. Investments or something."

" You are not quite as business-like as I thought you were, or you would have found out all that long ago. Shall I tell you what he has done with it ? "

" You ? What do you know about it ? "

" What do I know about it ? Oh, not much ; but I had dealings with him before now, my swell young lady. If he is your lord and master, I am——. No, I am talking nonsense ; I am half asleep, I think.

You go and call for Julius, and we'll have something short now."

"I will call Julius if you like, but I am not hungry; and I want to know, have you anything new to tell me about Claudius?"

"New? No, nothing."

"Then what were you talking about?"

"Talking about? Oh, nothing. I am an old man, and I wander sometimes." (Let it be understood that this old man "wandered" in an ineradicable Frankfort accent which would be tiresome as well as difficult to represent in phonetic spelling.)

"Have you lent him money?"

"Claudius Farringdon, Esq., of Sokebridge Manor? I have not lent him money. Have some schnapps? Julius!" The citizen of Rotterdam appeared. "Bring some glasses."

"*Ja!*"

"Now, my beautiful, aristocratic, and

ungrateful daughter, where are you going
to sleep?"

"I shall go to an hotel in Devonshire
Square, unless you will give me a bed
here."

"You shall have your mother's room.
The furniture is old, but it would fetch
fancy prices. But—I am only a hard-work-
ing poor old man."

"You want to be paid for the room?
Certainly. I would rather pay you than
take it for nothing. But about my proposition?"

"Oh, that? You come and talk to me
again about that when Claudius Farringdon
is dead. See if you're in the same mind
then."

"Why not now?"

"You don't seem to have found out your
own plans and things quite yet. When you
can plainly say what you want, perhaps I

can help you better. I can very likely get what I want out of the Farringdon lot without your help, without having you interfering in my business."

" All that is stupid. You think it caution; I call it obstinacy. You might even get the Manor House if I helped you. It was always your dream to be a country swell with a house ; and you'd be a magistrate too, and all sorts of things."

" Now look here," said the old man, "fen larks. What do you mean ? Am I to act in blind obedience to you ? No. Not good enough. But if you will stand in and do what you are told, I don't mind giving you a little commission."

Mr. Rosenfeld had not the slightest intention of letting his daughter go without making some judicious arrangement with her. He knew her temper of old too well not to know that if disappointed by him she was capable of taking any rash step in retribution which, considering her far too intimate knowledge of his affairs, might prove unpleasant, or at least inconvenient, for him. If anyone thinks his character impossibly, monstrously base, he need only study closely the contemporary history of meanness as displayed in our police and other courts, to be convinced that the achievements of human baseness are only surpassed by its aims; and that treachery, cowardice, and cupidity can descend as far as truth, courage, and love can ascend. Yet the poor fellows in the abyss can sometimes see the stars, if only reflected on the surface of the pitch in which they defile themselves.

" Well ? " said Jessica.

" I first knew Farringdon long ago in Germany, in the good old times when the tables were going. He did not waste much there ; no, not such a fool. But some of his friends did, and they introduced him to me. He was sharp! Oh, he was a beautiful man. You never saw his name backing a bill. When his friends lost and got cleaned out he cut them. When they wanted money he recommended them to come to me."

" Well ? "

" Well, well, well! You are in a hurry. You shall have your news, then, without any delay. He has left his house and a few hundreds a year to his son George. With the rest of his capital he has made an investment—I am speaking of years ago now, but it is all the same—he has bought an annuity for his life, and that's more than any of your foreign loans would give him, and safer too. And every penny he owns is spent on that annuity, and I suppose he spends every penny of the annuity in making himself comfortable ; yes, and getting you fine dresses. I wonder you ain't more grateful too."

Jessica's face was a study. If Claudius' face and a bottle of vitriol had been handy, the two might have come into sudden contact.

" And when he dies ? "

" You have—well, you have some pleasant recollections to fall back on. He owes you a debt of gratitude he never can repay, as he told me when he acknowledged a certain communication, and he doesn't mean to try to repay it. He says that when—some stupid thing out of a play, I forget—but when he is dead it won't much matter to him what happens to anyone else. He is a sharp man, a beautiful man ! "

" How do you know this is true ? "

" Because I managed the transaction for him."

" You bought his money, in short, and gave him the means to make his life the shorter."

" To make his life the shorter ; yes."

"And you did this knowing that it would one day suddenly leave me without a penny, without the slightest warning ?"

"Don't be angry, my dear; I meant to provide for you, if you behaved nice and business-like. I only told you this just to show you that you ain't much good without me to help you, as the income you expected will be spent by Mrs. George Farringdon on crocks and brass, and dresses and peacocks' tails, or whatever ladies do blue their money on now. Of course a beautiful young lady like you wouldn't be long, I daresay, in placing herself somehow. But you'd better stick to me, and I'll show you how to work this business. But don't you go to have any mysteries ; no kidding, you know. It takes more than one woman to best me." And they conversed for a long time in low tones.

After a time Julius Bloemendaal was

invited to join in the discussion when he
entered bearing a tray of glasses, and Mr.
Rosenfeld produced from the safe a square
bottle of gin. Jessica would not have any,
so Julius drank her share.

After that, and much bolting and locking,
they all retired—Jessica to the old bedroom,
with its sloping floor and frowsy atmosphere,
which had not been renewed for years, where
the dust lay on the furniture, and where the
bed had been made hurriedly by the worthy
Julius. And she lay awake nearly all night,
pursuing vivid streams of imagination to
startling and dramatic conclusions with that
excited clearness of mind peculiar to the
silent night-watches. At last she fell asleep,
this dark pretty woman, like a curled-up
cat in the large square bedstead, with her
dress and linen and lace strewed and scat-
tered carelessly all round the room, making
a strong contrast to its prim shabbiness. And

she smiled in her sleep. Whether she dreamed that she was playing with little " Yiddisher " boys in the free and easy manner of long ago, about Castle Street and Bevis Marks, or that she was administering hot retribution to the Farringdon family, is not known. But she smiled in her sleep. She almost purred.

Mr. Rosenfeld the elder did not pass a very comfortable night. The strange muddle of cunning, avarice, and superstition which formed his consciousness made him restless. Was his daughter going to revenge herself on him for some fancied wrong of long ago? Was it a fancied wrong? Had she any information she did not divulge? Was it really prudent to return her lead now, and trust to over-trumping her afterwards? What was the matter with her? She was angry with somebody. Who was it? Only the Farringdons? And if there were several people included in her wrath, was he one? Why?

Why not? He had not, perhaps, been the best of fathers; but the times were hard, and men had to be hard too, especially on those who might happen to be soft. But this embarrassing, incomprehensible, to him lady-like young woman, with rich garments, wafting about with her swinging skirts a faint atmosphere of vague perfumes of Araby, was not soft. She was hard, and he did not know how hard. Then there was that ungrateful young son of his—was there a plot between them to visit the sins of the parent on that parent, instead of letting them settle down in the hereditary fashion prescribed by the law? And many other equally groundless speculations passed through that apostolic old head as it lay moving uneasily on a dirty pillow. And it was very dark, and Mr. Rosenfeld thought he heard some one move in the next room where the safe was. He covered his head then with the bedclothes, no doubt in order to think what he had better do. Then his imagination, heated, no doubt, by the confined position, portrayed to him Julius Bloemendaal of Rotterdam, armed with pistols and daggers, blowing the safe open with dynamite, and copying all his private transactions in a fair text-hand at the table in the next room. This roused him to action, and he very cautiously and tremulously got out of bed, struck a silent lucifer, lit a tallow candle, and opened the parlour-door. Any robber who saw the grisly form of Mr. Rosenfeld senior in a night-shirt, holding a tallow candle crooked, must have thought himself "come for" before his time. Mr. Rosenfeld found nothing and nobody, as might have been expected, but made use of the opportunity to take, for purely medicinal purposes, another dose from that square bottle of schnapps. Then he went to bed and slept, and dreamed horribly. He dreamed very nasty dreams indeed, which made him wake up suddenly in a perspiration and strike matches.

Then he observed: " What a thing it is to be a parent! Such a lot of anxiety and everything! Go and have some more schnapps."

After this dose he slept sound.

CHAPTER V.

DICK STUDIES TWO PICTURES.

ABOUT twenty-four hours after his letter George Farringdon, his bride elect, and her relatives arrived at Sokebridge Manor. Kimburls had not been there before, nor his sister, nor his daughter. When they had journeyed south on previous occasions, their course had been limited by the latitude of London, where Claudius had seen and conversed with them on several occasions for the shortest time bare civility demanded. But on this occasion the latter was constrained to play the host—constant in courtesy, ready in conversation on subjects which did

not interest him, willing to walk or eat in
company when he wished to read and lounge
in solitude. The laird had got the fixed idea
into his slowly-working, but retentive mind
that Claudius Farringdon's strong point was
the pursuit of agriculture, and poured forth
long georgics, to the other's great tribulation,
on black bulls. Claudius disliked few subjects more, except commerce, Kimburls' alter-
native basis of discourse; and he went through
more self-sacrifice than he ever had done
before in those few long days which the laird
spent under his roof. He had not even the
consolation of satirising him before an ap-
preciative audience. Then Kimburls, in the
height of the delicate humour superinduced,
or at least intensified, by whisky, made sly
allusions to his sister setting her cap at
Claudius—witticisms which made the latter
gentleman's moustache droop limply, and
brought beads of cold sweat to his brow.

Jane Menteith herself cannot be said to have deserved these insinuations, as she spent most of her conversational powers in setting her brother right when he introduced his own reminiscences into conversation. George and Dick went out walking in the grounds and in the neighbourhood, and were pointed at and commented on by local critics. George rather liked being seen with her, being stared at, and being whispered about. Public opinion was a guiding factor in his theory of existence, however small the public, the opinion, yea, and the existence might be to other eyes than his. He was now proud, defiant, self-conscious. A Cæsar trailing a fair captive at his chariot's tail may have known this elation when he overheard the scarcely suppressed comment of the admiring Arrius among the crowd. Very likely he did, unaware that his right place would be at a cart's tail, with the ductile cowhide sinuously hovering in the immediate background. No doubt Arrius would have cheered with equal loudness at either procession, and made jests of equal delicacy.

George Farringdon appropriated the admiration and applause of the remote descendants of Arrius who beheld his lady's beauty, to his own glory, as the clown bows when the audience clap hands at the athlete.

Dick did not thoroughly enjoy all this. She was made unusually shy by the unusual nature of her position. She was confused by the number of influential families to whom it was found necessary that she should be exhibited, the wearisome iteration of mothers and daughters who scrutinised and criticised her, and poured out the same strictly correct conversation one after another, scrupulously denuded of originality, strictly modelled on precedent, strangely barren of ideas. She was made uncomfortable by the feeling that her father and aunt were making themselves

both tiresome and ridiculous to one who was
not so tolerant or of necessity partial as
George. She could not quite bring herself to
like Claudius. He often amused her, but she
was rather afraid of him, from some impression which she admitted to be vague and
ridiculous, but nevertheless failed to entirely
lose during her stay in the old brick house.
Being rather addicted to imaginative flights,
or, as her aunt put it, rather silly, just at
this period, she associated Claudius in some
mysterious manner with his house, giving the
latter a tinge of his personality. She had not
been in a house like it before, and its very
beauty of antiquity made it vaguely suggest
the owner hidden away in some recess of it
for a short hour's repose, perhaps, from the
boredom of unaccustomed hospitality. He
seemed of no particular age, a sort of house-
hold elf or tutelary demon or deity, who had
grown up with the structure and read queer

old books in it since the time, perhaps, of
Charles the Merry. And he said curious
things and looked curious things sometimes,
and she invested him daily more and more
with a sort of sulphurous halo. He rather
admired her, and was on the whole kind to
her after his fashion. He discovered that
this little girl, who would be his daughter-in-
law, was fond of books, and told her she
might read any of his she liked; "only," he
added, "if you feel curious about any with
which you are not already acquainted, I
advise you to consult me first. Don't consult
George; he doesn't know one from the
other."

"He does! he reads a great deal. He
often talks about books, Mr. Farringdon, your
books too."

"Yes; I know he does," replied Claudius,
with a dry smile. "And I respect you for
defending him, little girl." And he went

away. "So she thinks George is fond of reading," he mused afterwards. "I wonder how long he will succeed in keeping that idea up? However, it's their affair; and the sooner they settle the matter the sooner I shall be at peace."

Dick strolled round the library, with its strange, rare ornaments, exotic furniture, and quaint aromatic scents, and regarded the book-titles. She looked a strange contrast herself, in her fresh creamy print and lace summer dress and fair coiled-up hair, to the dim, heavy-aired, arras-hung haunt of a luxurious old hermit like her future father-in-law. She read a page here and there of certain old friends, and looked with some longing at the treasures in old vellum and brown calf, and with an indistinct apprehension and a kind of awesome curiosity at the prevailing yellow of the French department. And she sat in the chairs, trying and comparing them, to find which one was most comfortable. This was, of course, Claudius's own fireside one. Here she sat and looked about her, thinking dimly of a possible day when George might own this place and she would have it largely at her disposal—this part of it at any rate. She felt inclined to leave the outdoor possessions, such as the stables and the cattle, to take care of themselves, provided she might lurk among these books, or some of them, in a room whence she could see the sea and the trees. Many such and stranger dreams lurked in that deep armchair. The beauty of the place and its situation impressed her deeply, and tended to intensify her feeling for George. She looked at the gray-green flat foliage—masses of the great cedar overshadowing the little green lawn behind, where the warm afternoon sunlight of August revealed the livid lichenous gray shaft of the sun-dial, and made the grass-plot around it bright and tempting to straying feet.

She had escaped, as it were, from her relations for a short time, and George having gone out, he stated, to the stable, on some important quest, she had been left temporarily alone. Claudius did not want to be criticised by her too minutely, as he felt he would be in a *tête-à-tête*, where the new eyes of this young girl would notice tokens of infirmity about him, which an every-day spectator would miss. So he left her to enjoy solitude in his library. She occupied herself, as has been said, in a general tour of inspection. At last came the turn of the pictures. She was struck by the undeniable beauty of Sir Anthony Farringdon, and did not criticise the other qualities incompletely suppressed even in the work of a courtly and not too realistic painter, such as self-indulgent lips, straitened brain-space, and a general tone of what may be described as hard-softness in the expression—hard for others, soft for himself. All this she did not just at once discover. She only noticed that he was good-looking, that he had a pretty white-and-gold coat on, and that he resembled George. In a dark corner of the room another picture caught her eye, as she was walking over to examine a large blue jug, of German mediæval structure and immense height, which towered above her on a carved black stand of some solid heavy-looking wood. And she stood with one arm lightly caressing the base of the jug, with its dull blue-and-gray tracery of arms and allegories, and looked at the picture. It was small—about half life-size—and represented a woman, or rather the upper half of one, in an Eastern dress, with small gold coins strung across the forehead, and strong dark yellows and reds predominating in the fantastic but graceful dress. The colours certainly were loud, as loud as tambourines and triangles ; but they gave an undeniably appropriate setting to the strangely un-English face. It suggested languor, especially in the pose, which was one of reversion against a dull dirty-white plastered wall, which contrasted magnificently with the shapely exotic little head and its vivid costume. The whole figure leaned and lounged against this wall. The attitude was perfectly simple, such as any person might adopt who did not like the sustained exertion of unsupported up-rightness, and did not particularly seek after the poses which are a photographer's idea of grace. If all this meant languor, the beautiful, sullen, and disdainful mouth meant passion, maybe cruelty ; while the long dark eyes, with wan lids half closed, looked im-penetrably subtle, and expressed a high sen-suous potential. The skin was warmly and opaquely pale, rather like those Spanish skins unsurpassably described by De Musset. The face was rather long, the nose apparently straight, possibly aquiline.

Dick was startled by this face. It did not look friendly, but it looked inexplicably familiar, and strangely connected with some dream or some part of her past life; and she remained, fascinated by it, leaning on the black wooden stand, with the blue jar above her head, looking at this Oriental woman with the pale skin and level black brows. Then she looked back again at Sir Anthony, whose pretty, vicious, fragile face glanced into the room with arrogant and desirous eyes. Dick felt as if she had wandered into some enchanted den, where the atmosphere, the hangings, the fantastic garniture from Japan, China, Venice, Holland, Germany, Florence, Pompeii, and Regent Street, so diverse and yet so harmonious,

were all illusory, uncanny, and fearsome, that
it was just wildly possible that a certain old
wizard, with a spiky, iron-gray moustache
and a velvet jacket, might, by the use of
one of those old vellum books and some
of those strange and penetrating "drowsy
syrups" and fumigants, transform her to a
half-length picture, to be eternally hung between the white-and-gold young ancestor
and the mysterious Hadassar or Salome
flashing forth in the dim tapestried corner
opposite to him.

"Where have I seen you before, you
curious and pretty creature?" she almost
said aloud to the unknown portrait.

While she was wondering George came
in. He wore (on the premises) a suit of
flannels and a large flexible black felt broad
brim, which he delighted to curve and adjust
before a glass in private. Since that fancy-
dress ball in Glasgow Dick had seldom

thought him so like Sir Anthony up there
in the frame.   George looked at her with
wondering pale-blue eyes—fine large eyes
which faced you innocently and unmovedly,
like those of a blind man or the melancholy
variety of village natural.   Sir Anthony's,
however, were dark, like those of Claudius.

"I've been looking for you all over the
place. This is the place it last occurred to
me you might be in. Wouldn't you like to
come out?"

"Yes, if you like.   I've been looking
round at all the books and things.   Mr.
Farringdon very kindly told me I might.
What beautiful things there are here!"

"Regular palace of art—rather;" and he
glanced over his shoulder at a small rectan-
gular bevelled mirror in a flat brass frame
with branching candlesticks, to see if his
hair looked as it should, and surreptitiously
corrected the irregularities in it produced by

the act of taking off his hat. Then he
looked vaguely round the room, and halted
like a pointer before Sir Anthony, and
said :

"What do you think of him ? Come
here and look."

Dick came, and they stood together, he
with his arm round her, looking up at the
ancestor.

"He is handsome. Don't you wish you
could dress like that now, George ? You
would look splendid in that costume; and
then I could have brocaded trains and
powder, and you lace ruffles and a sword;
and we could dance a minuet and a gavotte
in the hall, with the lamp high up above
and reflected in that shining dark floor."

"Yes. Do you know, some of the
people about here find a kind of resemblance
to me in that fellow's picture ?"

George had a way of sometimes ignoring

intervening conversation until he had fully got rid of any point that might be occupying his own mind—usually one of a purely subjective character. Some people were made irritable by this habit, especially if three or four talking together were several topics ahead of George and the first instalment of his rather vague and partially - expressed verdict on some other topic, when it occurred to him to give the rest to a world that was not waiting for it. It gave the impression that he had not listened, which is always unsatisfactory to participants in a conversation.

But Dick forbore to be impatient, and took for granted that George's ideas were more important than her own, and felt gently rebuked, as if she had somehow said something silly.

"It is rather like you, certainly."

"I thought you would see it."

M 2

"George, who is that ? Is it a portrait ?"

Dick turned round, directing his attention to the other picture.

"That ? Oh, that is a fantastic fanciful sort of thing it pleased the governor to get once. He thought it reminded him of some-one he knew, I believe."

"It seems to remind me vaguely of some-one I know. I was trying to think whom just when you came in."

"Curious. Well, look here : I have to inform you that there will be some people here this afternoon—to tea, you know—and I want you to show yourself. By-the-way, one of them is an old acquaintance, Charlie Deane. We don't know them very intimately, but there has always been a certain friendship between the families. You see, they are quite well-born people, although they are hard up."

"Oh, I'm so glad to hear that ! He has

an aunt and a cousin—yes, and a grandmother, hasn't he?"

"Yes; two first are coming with him.
How did you know?"

"He told me; I happened to remember
it. And now—yes! now I know whom
that picture reminds me of. It is that Mr.
Rosenfeld, who was with Charlie Deane in
Schlangenberg."

George had long ago seen the resemblance.
He replied:

"By Jove! so it does, now you mention
it. As that is a picture by a French artist—
probably from a model in Paris or Algiers,
or somewhere—I can't account for it."

"You didn't like Mr. Rosenfeld, did
you?"

"I don't think we were calculated to get
on remarkably well together. I believe we
thought differently on most subjects. Besides,
he was a Jew. I'm not prejudiced against

Jews. They have their uses; but I bar them in society."

"You asked him to our wedding, didn't you?"

"Oh, yes; but then one asks everybody and anybody to a wedding."

"I don't see why one would."

"Neither do I. I'd much rather not; but it's the right thing to do, and people expect it. Besides, every one who is asked has to give a present. Comes in useful."

"If we could furnish a house exclusively with travelling-clocks and sets of dessert knives and forks—yes. I wish people didn't give presents, and dinners, and breakfasts, and all that. Oh, George! *must* we be married before all this crowd of people, who don't know or care about me, and will make remarks to each other in low voices and laugh? I'm getting so tired and frightened of it all. And you know I've no one but you to consult; so you must tell me what is best. It is no use talking to father or Aunt Jane; they have made up their minds, and are peacefully determined never to unmake them. I can't help being shy, though it may be silly."

"Ought to get over that. Why, how are people married in Scotland? I mean respectable people?"

"At home. The minister comes to their house, and a few friends are there——"

"And a few broth, and a few toddy after —I know. Well, we do these things otherwise in England. I daresay we shall get over the ordeal. In the meantime come and walk about out of doors."

And George Farringdon removed his bride-elect from the baleful glance of that shadowy suggestion of Caspar Rosenfeld up in the corner, with her glances of invitation, of defiance, and lazy subtlety at the white-coated cavalier. She seemed to laugh at them all.

"I believe those two get down from their pictures at night," said Dick, "and play cards, and then Sir Anthony sings, and the lady plays a tambourine. I should think she could dance, too, if she chose to take the trouble. Sir Anthony would sing some of the old Jacobite songs, as we used to, you know, when we were children, at the cave-period, as Professor MacGillivray used to say, of our existence, when you were the Young Chevalier, and I Flora MacDonald. And perhaps she sings with him; and when the cock crows, and the day dawns, they go back. I suppose they have to get on chairs to do that."

"Governor ought to know. He is generally there till dawn, reading and smoking."

"George, I'm afraid you're not romantic."

"Dick, I'm afraid you are. No, I admit

I'm not. Romance is all very well for children, and poets and painters, and people who lived ever so long ago, when men wore picturesque clothes, but it doesn't suit me. All the romance in my life has been put into it by you, Dick. I go in for realism and analysis."

"The people who write novels seem to find there is still something left in this century to talk about."

"Mostly women, and they talk mostly sentimental rot. The only novels worth reading, as giving a true view of life as it is, are the French naturalists."

" Are they the best ? "

" They are the truest and the most interesting."

" Are they better and truer than Walter Scott, or any of the English and Scotch novels written now ? "

" Certainly. None of that picturesque

affectation and sentimentality about them. They mean business."

"Will you let me have one or two to read? You know I don't know much about foreign literature, so you must educate me."

"Let you read naturalistic novels? Not quite. Ladies don't read them."

"Don't they? Well, perhaps they are right. But ladies *can* read Scott, and Dickens, and Thackeray, and Reade, and Besant, and Black, so I suppose I must stick to picturesqueness and sentimentality. But do you like reading books I mustn't read?"

Here they reached the secluded shade of a cedar-tree, and sat on a bench concealed from public view.

"Never mind discussing literature now," said George, "and give me a kiss."

They and the cedar and the grass-grown ground made a very pretty group indeed.

" But, George ? "

" Well ? "

" Isn't this sentimentality ? "

" Oh, shut up ! "

CHAPTER VI.

IN ILLYRIA AGAIN.

IT was one of those warm, bright days in August, when London looks perhaps at its best—a time selected to leave it by certain who call themselves Society, whom irreverent statistical science calls, I believe, the Floating Population. If the minute congeries of assimilated units, self-termed Society, knew how very pleasant certain London seasons are when they are not there, they might perhaps stay longer. Perhaps some of them, in their secret souls, do know very well indeed what London is like in August and September after all, though they keep the knowledge of these mysteries to themselves. This may or may not be. At any rate, it may be safely said that though there was a block in what the papers called the "vehicular traffic" in Holborn, though every form of business went on as usual, though the theatres were crowded, and the pavements black with hurrying human millions, there was Nobody in town. And nobody seemed to miss the distinguished somebodies who were not in town.

Caspar Rosenfeld threw down his pen impatiently, and went and sat in his open window to listen to the distant roar of the tide of London life, and to watch the changing tone of the leaves in the few melancholy trees which adorn that restful, ancient, and quaint courtyard of Barnard's Inn. He was not much disturbed about the empty days spent by waiters in Pall Mall clubs while their august employers, many of them British legislators, were killing the smaller and less formidable varieties of wild beast and fowl on moor and main. He took a letter out of his pocket and re-read it. That morning he had had a dream. He was walking on the Thames Embankment in the evening, towards an immense, vague, and beautiful building veiled in warm yellow sunlight mist. He knew by the independent intuition of a dream that this was the Palace of Westminster, and was not in the least surprised to observe that instead of its stones being gray, they were red. The red palace and the sunset mingled in one gloriously confused reflection in the water, such as only may be seen in dreams or in Venice. There was not a human being near, nor were there any boats on the water. He was not at all surprised at the fact, and accounted for it scientifically by observing, "It must be the Boat-race."

Which, for a dream, is not on the whole a bad piece of reasoning. And he saw coming towards him, out of that indescribable and splendid composition of sunlight, mist, architecture, colour, and water—Dick Menteith, alone, and apparently expecting to see him there. He remembers that they had a long conversation, that she told him the marriage with Farringdon was all a delusion, and that they were going together to open Parliament, and she had come to ask him to write her her Queen's Speech. And she laughed and cried, and clung to him as he kissed her eyes and hair. And then he wrote the Queen's Speech, there on a piece of paper, on the flat-topped embankment balustrade, looking out over the river towards—towards the vine-clad Traubenberg, with the white gleaming road below, where the peasants led their carts slowly through the dust. And he wrote, she leaning over his shoulder, "My

Lords——" She took the pen from him, and it grew dark, while the palace remained glowing red, outlined on the blackness of chaos. She wrote in the air. "When the rain comes," she said, "you will see it." The rain came, and they stood together under it. And the thunder came. And they stood together under it. And the Speech she wrote on air came out in blue Gothic lightning letters; and he could not read it, and woke, murmuring:

"God help me! Dreaming of what might have been. God help you! For it was too good to be."

A letter had been thrust under the door by his laundress, who was laying breakfast in the adjoining room. It was the letter he now, towards evening, read again, with the calm, warm, western light slanting in at the window and revealing the worm-worn frailty of its woodwork. The letter was a fair enough sequel to the dream to illustrate the truth of a well-known saying concerning the relation between dream and fact.

It was from Charlie Deane, and below are its contents :

"Sokebridge, Aug. 28.

"C.D. C.R., *salutem dicit.* We are all right. Hope you are. Beastly hot; almost as hot as Schlangenberg. I immerse daily in sea. G.M." (Charlie's hieroglyph for grand-mamma) "says I've improved by the tour. Said I hadn't noticed much difference myself. She wishes me to record her gratitude to you for the parental care you've taken of me, and hopes I wasn't much trouble. I forbore to tell her the trouble and caretaking were largely on my side. We, *i.e.* Aunt Lucy, Lily, and self, went to call on the Menteiths and Farringdons, etc., a day or two ago, and had afternoon tea. We saw

Miss D. M. first; she and Lily took to each other immensely, which surprised me, as they are so different.

"Then G. Farringdon turned up, having evidently been spending the time in dressing himself prettily, and scenting his handkerchief with chypre, which I abhor. She — Miss D. M.—then asked me how and where you were, and casually, quite casually, remarked that you and I were expected at her wedding, appealing to G. F. for corroboration. He looked rather thunderous, but caved in and confirmed the invitation with a sort of gloomy cordiality, adding, however, that he was rather puzzled where to put you up, as the house was pretty full. I relieved, and I trust annoyed him by saying we were going to entertain you. Miss D. M. was much obliged, and looked it. So you have got to come, respected sir, and that right soon. Wedding on the 1st; come any day before

'that—there are only three, but send message
first. We are all longing for you, especially
my aunt, who admires you very much. Lily,
whose cheek is unbounded" (chaotic interval),
"and who is now looking over my shoulder
and making me blot and sputter as above,
indulges herself in the hope that you will
write a book about her, and is pestering
her guardians for a peacock-blue velvet dress,
with which to dazzle and dismay your critical
eye. An attic has been swept and garnished
for you. Lily has now inserted a penholder
down the back of my neck, and a scrimmage
has ensued, so farewell."

Caspar repocketed the letter and walked
about the room, finally settling in a chair
and staring into the empty fireplace, his
legs stretched out before him, his hands in
his pockets, his shoulders high, a short pipe
still in the corner of his mouth, where it

had been, intermittently, since breakfast. He had no coat nor waistcoat on, nor collar, and his hair was hanging about his forehead. The table was occupied by books, paper, some unwashed breakfast apparatus, and a tabby kitten, who was minutely investigating a tobacco-pouch, with an expression of strong disapprobation.

A knock came at his door, heralding the entrance of two men. The first was Mr. Jack Miller, notable, as usual, for an expression of calm self-convinced superiority to all terrestrial beings, produced by a long contemplation of them and of himself, particularly of the latter, held as a vital and consoling faith, and externally proclaimed by a tendency to walk with his nose and chin uplifted. Mr. Miller usually succeeded in irritating Caspar by his tendency to despotic utterances on things social, artistic, and literary, in which strict accuracy was

subordinated to a certain quality called smart-
ness. Mr. Miller, having demolished, to his
own satisfaction, all objects usually deemed
worthy of veneration, placed himself on the
unoccupied pedestal, and invited worshippers.
As far as the practical results of his art were
concerned the worshippers remained coy.
But there was a small sect, mainly feminine,
who did to some extent share in the cult.
He dressed with a view to economy and
picturesqueness combined, and was a great
believer in strangely-tinted silk handkerchiefs
and velveteens. Part of the present artistic
style consisted of a crop of long hair, to
which he paid great attention, and on account
of which he gained much derision. It was
certainly a cheap adornment, accessible to
the poorest. This, however, had only become
apparent since he had known Caspar, which
gave strong grounds for suspicion that it
was an imitation of the latter's. It was

also attributed to his habit of rapturously adoring the fifteenth-century Italian painters, and their nineteenth-century English rivals; and opinion was divided among his friends as to whether he really did admire them, or merely gave way to the modern temptation to be eccentric. He still continued to pour quotations from his favourite poets on any one who would listen, in and out of season. Caspar, whose knowledge of literature included everything Jack Miller wholly or partially knew, as the German Ocean includes the Thames Sewage—as Miller himself gracefully remarked one day, in a state of mingled wrath and humiliation—occasionally inflicted signal discomfiture on Miller, when he ventured into the vast world of the unknown, and trifled with its terminology with the air of a connoisseur.

Well, he was as he was made. A few

liked him and a many did not. His companion was observing as they entered:

"Bar your chiaroscuro and flake-white, you're a very ignorant man, Miller. Now see, I'm forty-two. If you carry your years with the grace and sprightliness, mingled with dignity, which I do, when you're that age—well, you'll be a holy show. And that's truth."

And the speaker gave his hat a touch more in the direction affected and profanely nicknamed by the cavaliers of old, turned up his long, grizzly-brown moustache, adjusted his glasses on his nose, and laughed at Miller a defiant wrinkled laugh. His hands, plunged in his trousers-pockets, pushed back laterally the skirts of a time-honoured frock-coat, which was known in more than one European and Asiatic capital. His trousers were a little frayed at the feet, his boots showed signs of wear. He looked what he was, an irreclaimable Irish Bohemian, who considered it no reproach to be such. And a more keen and careless-tongued, adventurous, child-loving, reckless, generous, happy-go-lucky, picturesquely-shabby good fellow never walked Fleet Street, or "stood" a friend a meal or a drink. Should he read these lines, he will have the liberality to forgive the necessarily inadequate representation of his many amusing and endearing qualities.

"It is you, is it, O'Rourke? What is your news? How are you, Miller?"

"Isn't he a picture?" observed O'Rourke, standing contemplatively by Caspar, his head critically on one side, his hat more so.

"Jingle in the Fleet," suggested Miller, flicking his leg with a switch. "Why this thusness, Rosenfeld?"

"If you mean why am I partially dressed, because it is a hot day. I sit here because

I am tired. I am tired because I've been writing magazine verses which express a state of mind exactly the reverse of my own, which is unfit for publication."

"Why don't you come out? Nonsense sticking in here on a day like this. There's a gaudy sunset coming on out in the direction of the Marble Arch."

"I don't care. I have not your mono-mania for sunsets in Oxford Street. Besides, there are likely to be plenty more where that came from if I should hanker after one at any time."

"Come and have a drink," said O'Rourke.

"I don't feel inclined to come out, or to have a drink. What do you two want?"

"Wanted to see you, and hear all about you. You've been missed by me. Miller tried to bait me in your celebrated style by making derogatory remarks about Ireland and the borra I'm going to represent; but it has not the flavour of your patent unrivalled exhilarating misanthropy and soothing non-intoxicating pessimism."

"This is not the place to compose extempore leaders, O'Rourke."

"Why haven't you been to see us?" asked Miller. "Our *ménage* has been increased by a bull-terrier and a black kitten, both in their first childhood; and Rosa's rapidly going into her second over them. We are a merry family."

"No doubt. But if a merry family will live in Brixton, they can't expect a person of my busy habits to get there often. Besides, I've only been in England a few days, I believe."

"Where have you been—Paris?"

"No, Germany."

"Have a good time?"

"Oh yes. Spent most of my present available cash. *The Investigator* has been unusually dilatory in sending me the periodic cheques too."

"And they have had reams of your copy, as I have noticed, the last two or three weeks. You have been pungent lately. That's partly what we came to talk about; but it was nearly put out of my head by a yarn of this man's, to the effect that two hundred and fifty per cent. of the English army were Irishmen, which was another apology for the fact that——"

"Oh, bother!" interrupted O'Rourke. "You take too many words to say too little. It just means landlords are in season again, and good bags are expected. About you and *The Investigator*, the matter is that it has changed hands. The new proprietor is ostensibly one Dr. Van Westerdijk, though he is no doubt backed by some anonymous capitalist. He doesn't look a typical Crœsus himself."

"Foreigner?"

"A London foreigner. I don't know any good of him. He is not often at the office. They have got a new editor; Jew, I think: in fact, it is in their hands, rather. The rest they are going to keep on. Saunders is there as usual, and Skinner and Moriarty, and that lot."

"Doesn't much matter to me as long as they pay, and that soon."

"They don't do it soon," said O'Rourke. "I had a couple of columns there two or three weeks back, and had to go and freeze on to the place for four hours to get it. 'Tisn't like what it used to be in poor old Wilkins's time. Westerdijk is a low Jew baste. I beg your pardon, Caspar, but he is. What I also meant to tell you was as I'd had a row with him—never mind why, or I shall get into a nest of circumlocutious parentheses no human power could extricate me from, and there I shall remain in a sort of extra circle, say the Upper Circle of the Inferno, crawling through a tortuous sentence for all eternity. The fact is——"

"Begin again."

"This same proprietor, Westerdijk, also runs a lucrative Society weekly, with illustrations. Miller does some of them, d—d badly too. Now I'm in his list of the lost, his 'Index Expurgatorius,' for all time, because—well, I expostulated with him mildly on a purely personal matter; in fact, I nearly knocked his ugly head off with a cane chair; but that's a matter of detail. As no one knows of this yet, it occurred to me you might fill my place on this Society rag. The catastrophe only came off a little while back; I bet they'd take copy with your name to it without reading. You seem to want to waffle in the spondoolicks just now. Here's your chance."

"Isn't it cutting away your ground in any way?"

"Not a bit. I'm busy on one daily, and have sold the non-existent Irish right of a lot of old mag. stories, and am engaged to fake up some new East-end stuff—docks and Chinese, and all that. You send them a serial story."

"If Ireland were populated by O'Rourkes," said Caspar, "it would be, if possible, more of an earthly paradise than it is at present. Thank you, old man; I'll act on your hint. As you observe, I'm impecunious just now, and am writing off my quarter's rent in magazine verse. I must get some man to share these rooms or quit them, I'm afraid. Look here, O'Rourke, I don't know that making amiable speeches was ever a practice of mine. You'll have to do without that; but you understand I am much obliged to you, and am thankful to find in Illyria the human kindness which is very scarce out of it."

"All right," said the kind-hearted Irishman. "*Vive la Bohème!* I only hope you won't have a row with any of these sweeps of compatriots of yours."

"I can't afford to have a row."

"Why don't you get a partner in here?" asked Miller. "It would halve the cost of the diggings."

"Haven't got a partner. Never had. Don't know that I want to." After a pause Caspar added: "I beg his pardon. I have a partner in my eye."

"Have him in your rooms," said Miller.

"You University chaps," said O'Rourke, "always say rooms. It's a perfect shibboleth. It takes years to teach an ex-University man to say chambers or apartments."

"Heaven defend me from calling the

place I live in, however humble, apartments!" replied Miller.

"The word implies solitude," said
O'Rourke. "Originally, apartment signified
a room you meant to be apart in. What
apart meant we know from stage directions."

"Lord, Lord!" misquoted Miller, "how
these old men are given to this vice of
punning! How ill a pair of glasses and a
post on a penny daily become a fool and a
jester!"

"I've had more than a pair of glasses,
and will gladly take another at your expense.
And mine is not a penny post. That was
Sir Rowland Hill. You're a very ignorant
man, Miller."

"So you have said before."

"When you two have done gibing at
each other," observed Caspar, "perhaps you
will tell me the name of this Society paper
and its whereabouts?"

"It is called *The Lamp*, and its slaves send their contributions to Key Court."

"Thanks."

"Dress yourself, man, and come out and look on the daylight while you can, and have a drink."

"Thanks, O'Rourke. But I told you I don't feel inclined to come out, or to have a drink."

"What's the matter?"

"Work's the matter. If I'm to do something for this Fleet Street night-light, I must do it. I can't be sure that I've anything near enough completion to send in."

"You're very laconic and matter-of-fact to-day. What's wrong?"

"Oh, nothing! Nothing you can put right."

"Look here, old pal; if you want a quid or two, I've got a little to spare. It isn't much, because I've got the detached villa

in Brixton next to this painter-chap, with
water-rates, and a wife and child waiting
for me inside it; but don't be offended at
my offer.   It isn't often I've a chance of
making such.   Generally the other way."

"O'Rourke, if there can be an angel in
drab shorts and gaiters, as Mr. Weller states,
I have no hesitation in saying there is one
in a shady frock-coat and black-rimmed
glasses.   But I'm not distressed immediately
that way.   And I will come out with you
and have a drink."   And Caspar went into
his bedroom to make himself presentable.

"What's it mean, do you think?" said
O'Rourke to Miller.

"If it was any other man I should say he
was in love or in liquor, but Rosenfeld——"

"Is not such a fool.   Very funny, isn't
it, all this impecuniosity business?"

"Very," replied Miller rather drily, thinking of Rosa's threatened sealskin.

"I know a man, soldier too, has danced *vis-à-vis* to that old skunk Metternich, at Vienna, and had to pawn his orders to get breakfast."

"I am ready now," said Caspar, reappearing in his usual outdoor attire.

"Come on, then," said O'Rourke. "I'll take you to a place where you'll meet a circus-clown and a strong man."

"Take me where you like. A lamb on its way to the butcher is violent resistance compared to my docility. By-the-way, Miller, you are about my size—can you lend me a black Sunday coat for a day or two?"

"Oh, yes; come down home with me to-night, and you can carry it off. What are you going to do?"

"I'm invited to a wedding, and—I'm afraid I must go."

"Not your own?" observed O'Rourke, in a note of alarm.

o 2

Caspar laughed.

"I should not dress up for that, I fancy."

"I didn't know. I thought you looked depressed."

Part the Fifth.

MARRIAGE AND DEATH AND DIVISION.

CHAPTER I.

A mannikin stood in a wedding dress ;
My love stood by him, and both said, Yes ;
A thousand laughing devils echoed the loud Amen.

IT was a brilliant morning, the 1st of September, when the white convolvulus clambered round the stalks of growing grain, and was duly anathematised by the farmers for so doing ; when the first faint yellow leaves were falling, herald flakes of the many-coloured floor, which later would be brown and crimson and umber on all the paths, and rotten, black, and ruinous in mould-pits at last. The annual *transit gloria terræ* was beginning. The air was still, the sun hot, the sky blue and

hazy, the sea glittering with the many-facetcd
ever-moving ripples, which laughed at poor
Prometheus, and have laughed and scowled
alternately ever since. The summer was
going, the woods were dying, and Dick
Menteith was being dressed for her wedding.
Caspar and Charlie were sauntering on
the green edge of the cliff, in black coats
and tall hats, waiting rather impatiently for
the time when they should enter the large,
new, and extremely fashionable church where
the wedding was to take place.

Caspar's face was transformed by the
sunlight into a white mask with black shadows
on it, as he stood " on the brow o' the
sea," following with his eyes a white gull as
it flew over the far-spread Channel into the
place where sea and sky met indistinctly
separable in a band of gray-blue haze.
Charlie would have been cheerful enough,
but for a certain nervous anxiety. He was

disgusted and irritated about the marriage, and his mind was uneasy about Miss Lily Carew, the mysterious workings of that young person's emotional centre, if she had one, being a constant puzzle—a charm to his eyes and ears at one moment, and a simple provocation to his temper at the next. And he thought he might legitimately use Caspar as a convenient object whereon to discharge the meditations of his troubled mind. So he suddenly said :

" I don't think I can stand all this much longer."

" All which ? " said the other, turning round with a wan smile.

" Well, first of all, this church and break-fast business. What's the use of you loafing about stretched on a spiritual rack, making spasmodic jokes at intervals ? O man ! drop it. It's not too late. We can smash the whole pitiful concern between us. Look here, if you will undertake the Young Lochinvar part, I will do my best to help ; and once you have declared war and love you will find we can see all the Farringdons and Kimburls at the devil!"

"Nonsense!"

"It isn't nonsense, though it may not be expressed with the coherence of a *Times* leader. And, by Jove! I'd make it into a *parti carré*; if I only could once manage it nothing in the world should part us then."

Caspar trembled. "And suppose I don't want to bring about any such result in my own case?"

"I can't suppose so when I see that you would give your very life for a girl, who is going to throw herself away innocently on that gowk, George Malcolm Farringdon. It is so pitiful!"

"He is not a gowk. He is her affianced

husband ; and if ever man loved woman he does. And she likes him in her peaceful way. Don't talk to me any more about that. You know I cannot help it, or carry out quixotic Gretna Green escapades. Drop the subject, I don't like it. Let's go and see the opening farce."

And they walked towards the church, while nursery-maids wondered and said : " That's 'im ! " Near the church - porch juvenile gazers with pipes of clay smoked and spat, and laughing in the cacophonous manner peculiar to the British lout, observed, " Lardydar, that's 'im ! " They subsequently made the same remark of any decently-dressed male who appeared.

" All this sort of thing tends to set off the solemnity of these occasions," said Caspar to Charlie, as they wandered round the inside of the building looking for a seat. They mixed with the crowd near the east end.

Then there appeared two young gentlemen from Oxford, friends and supporters of Farringdon, with kid gloves, and camellias and maidenhair in their button-holes.

Then appeared Farringdon, handsome and excited, resembling more than ever the young man who fought for the white cockade. The nursery-maids liked him, and said he was " ever so much 'andsomer than the first one with the black back'air."

Then there was a great deal of waiting, as well as fidgeting with hats on the part of the two young gentlemen from Oxford. The minutes lingered. Then a kind of murmur in the crowd, such as is heard at the firing of a bouquet of rockets, only more subdued, made Caspar shut his eyes and shiver. When he opened them again Dick Menteith, in a white satin dress and white lace veil, was passing before him on the arm of a very elegant old man with a beautiful figure and waxed iron-gray moustache.

She did not see Caspar. She only saw the confused crowded dazzle which a stage novice sees on the rising of the curtain.

Charlie had disappeared into the crowd to speak to his relations, who were present as mere spectators. Claudius Farringdon looked like an elderly Mephistopheles as he smiled into his hat for a few seconds, in reverent conformity with aristocratic church usages. He had gone through a great deal that morning. He had first of all been obliged to get up much earlier than usual, and dress himself in a way in which he did not usually dress except when in town. Then he had listened politely to the conversation of Mr. Menteith of Kimburls, on the Commaircial Treaty dispute, during a considerable part of the morning. But it was a consolation to him to feel that he was, next to the Happy Pair (as the local paper subsequently called them), the most imposing and conspicuous person present. He could not quite understand why the soles of his feet had a kind of woolly feeling, or why he sometimes lifted them so high in walking. That had bothered him a good deal lately. He hoped he was not going to get worse. He did not see the tall, brown-outlined figure of Mrs. Brandon, far off against a white stone pillar, with her dark impenetrable eyes fixed on him, with a half-smile on that face that might have descended in a direct line from the Serpent of old Nile. Nor did he see the eye-glass of the little medical student, Charlie Deane (whom he scarce knew by sight), peering curiously at that occasional high-stepping action of his, and muttering, "Patient feels as if he were walking on balls of worsted. Yes, respected sir, we shall hear from you soon, I think, advertising for a permanent situation in Hades."

"What?" said Lily, who was trying to see the bride through the numerous human bodies which intercepted the view.

"Nothing. Hush! They are beginning the service."

It took a vicar and two curates to make George Farringdon and Dick Menteith man and wife. Caspar noticed that the vicar "shied" (as Charlie subsequently expressed it) at the name "Richard" as applied to a lady. And he wondered why he felt himself inclined to laugh.

Kimburls and his sister—the other parties to the transaction—were, of course, there : the former in his best broadcloth—not new, of course, but what he wore on the Sabbath-day at home ; the latter in a lavender silk of antique design, which made a great deal of noise, certainly not describable by the rather soothing word *froufrou*. She had worn it first at her brother's wedding, and will, no doubt, be prepared to wear it, dyed, at his funeral. It served to set off the manly dignity of her person very effectively.

The vicar read St. Paul's exhortation to

married persons, and took the opportunity to
add a few remarks of his own, to the visible
annoyance of the congregation, who began to
tramp noisily out.

And then Caspar's mind's eye wandered
to the solitary chambers in Barnard's Inn,
where he sat one summer afternoon, not so
long ago, in an armchair on one side of the
fireplace, looking at another one, empty, on
the other, and fancying a small, fair head,
nestling in its cushioned back, with quiet
eyes smiling at him in the way eyes smiled
before sorrow came into the world, in far-off
days that never were, which some men have
loved to dream of in their great, loving,
and pitiful hearts, that joyed with the
joyous (whose joys they shared not), and
pitied the sad and sinning, because they
had sorrowed and sinned themselves. And
he saw the small hands pour out tea for
him, and search wonderingly through his

books, and heard the voice make playful comments on what he wrote, satirise and worship him all the while—the same gentle voice he had just heard say " I will !" to the question that fixed her fate for bad or good. He saw a large straw-and-satin white-feathered hat—always the same one—thrown carelessly on his table among pens and books and pipes, and he knew that the deep gulf, reaching from the abyss to the stars, which separated him from so many human sympathies might have been stepped over then and filled up for ever, and the bitterness of life made sweet for him so long as life lasted. And with all this he felt a great ferocious joy, greater than that Scævola felt with his hand in the brazier. For Scævola, if he ever existed, had a pit and gallery to play to, which probably was a source of satisfaction to him.

Caspar Rosenfeld felt that he scared his soul before the solitary and eternal eyes of

God, " unless," as he reflected, " the universe goes on passionless Juggernaut wheels of its own, in which case I'm, perhaps, making an Altruistic ass of myself." Then the organist (a local amateur) suddenly crashed and pealed out that exulting " Wedding March," which has turned the old days to derision to so many ears before now, and the principal characters of the foregoing drama filed out.

Then there was a breakfast at Sokebridge Manor, of course. At this, as has been previously intimated, Caspar and Charlie were guests, and were each placed beside some ordinary tolerably pretty and tolerably silly girl of the neighbourhood. Charlie's neighbour said to him, in the lull of noise after a much-applauded, elegant, and epigrammatic address from Claudius, " What is the matter with your friend? He looks as if he had lost something."

"Perhaps he has," replied Charlie, and changed the subject.

It is not necessary to state at any length the facts that the vicar delivered an impressive, mildly jocular discourse, "coupling with it the name of his friend and former pupil, George Farringdon," who replied that he was aware he was taking away a treasure beyond his deserts ("which," Charlie remarked in an aside to his partner, "is true"); or that Kimburls was what he called "wetty" in the Glaswegian tongue; or that one of the young gentlemen from Oxford emitted several rather dislocated remarks, in which Hymen, the Graces, and the bridesmaids got very much mixed up, terminating with the facetious sentence he had surreptitiously pencilled in the fly-leaf of his prayer-book in church, "got up" ever since, and remembered perfectly—all but the point—at the critical moment. It was all very weary and dreary.

At least it seemed particularly so to Claudius Farringdon, who wanted a comfortable chair, a cigar, a laughter-provoking book, and solitude as an antidote to the superfluity of fatherly emotion he had been compelled, by the *convenances*, to display all the morning, and to Caspar, who wanted to be alone with the sea and the sky and himself.

At last he and Charlie were released, and walked silently back to the bijou residence, where Caspar retired to Charlie's room, which commanded the garden. There he sat in the open window, reading to himself some " chronicle of wasted time," and looking across the dark-green fir-tops beyond the garden into space, while Charlie was giving his relatives an account of the breakfast, and displaying a small fragment of mottled black matter, with a yellowish-gray cortex, which he asserted to be a portion of the cake he had brought for Lily. That damsel ate it forthwith, and proceeded to ask where Mr. Rosenfeld was. Whereat her cousin, Mr. Charles Deane, chid her for devouring the whole of the cake herself; and a short and merry war ensued, in the midst of which the noise of wheels was heard in the road in front of the house. This was the carriage returning from the railway station. George Farringdon and his wife were just then in a first-class compartment, accompanied by some very new-looking leather-covered dressing-cases, bags, and umbrellas, a travelling clock, several Society and illustrated papers, *en route* for Paris.

"She seems almost too young to be married," said Miss Deane.

"I don't know," said Charlie. "She is older in some ways than you'd think."

"If she's too young she'll grow older in the course of a few years, most likely," remarked Lily, with a certain pertness which is occasionally displayed by young girls, more especially towards their near relatives.

"We've argued all about her and him over and over again," she continued, "and repeated the same things to one another till I'm sick of it."

"If you are as well-behaved, as well-read, and as nice and kind as Dick Menteith—Farringdon, I mean—at her age," said Miss Deane, "we shall all rejoice, I'm sure, and I shall feel my trouble in bringing you up has not been entirely thrown away."

Lily laughed.

"Wasn't I an awful little pest to educate, Aunt Lucy?"

"Well, to put it candidly, dear, you were. I suppose most children are, and that you were not worse than the rest; but, you see, you came to us almost wild, and wanted to pray to a hideous little silver Spanish saint some servant or some one had given you in the benighted place you were born in ; and you got into fearful passions, and said awful things in Spanish, which I'm glad to say I didn't understand, and which I'm more glad to say you've forgotten."

" I was one of your earliest victims," said Charlie. "Being a small boy, I was ordered about like any amount of slaves. I was directed to climb trees to get you eggs, and cones, and funguses, and various other articles of scientific interest. I had to descend with eggs in my mouth, in awful peril of swallow- ing them ; and if one broke down my œsophagus, as did once happen, and not a nice egg either, you laughed consumedly and did a war dance round the tree."

" I'd like to do it again, too," replied Lily. " I know I should destroy my dignity and my dress, but I'd like to go bird's-nesting this very afternoon."

" I regret to say that birds do not build

nests in September, much, unless due notice is given beforehand that they will be required. It is not usual. But you can worship a *gri-gri* if you like."

"I suppose you think that awfully clever," retorted Lily, who was not easily "sat on."

"I more than think it. You might come and fish for efts and bully-heads too in stagnant ponds and running brooks. That was one of your great juvenile amusements when you had ceased to worship idols. But it is risky work for a young person in her seventeenth year, with heels and a skirt, which, though with all the brevity allowed by decorum, is evidently very tight."

"Dr. Johnson says, 'The man who resorts to personality, and considers it wit, should be an object of deserved scorn—and several other things—to everybody.'"

"Does he, indeed? And does he finish his sentence as artistically as that?"

" I'm going out," concluded Lily, without noticing Charlie's last dab; "it's far too fine an afternoon to stay poking about the house."

And she disappeared, snatching a knitted black Tam o' Shanter bonnet of Charlie's from a peg in the passage, for the better protection of her head.

Mrs. Deane came into the room, bearing a bag which contained all the apparatus needed by a perpetual knitter, including an unfinished pair of socks, destined for Charlie's winter wear.

" Where is your friend Mr. Rosenfeld, Charlie?" said she.

" Upstairs, grandma; he's writing letters, or reading, or something. He's in my room. There's plenty of tobacco there, and a copy of Shakespeare, so he can't lack occupation."

" Go and see him, dear, and ask him if he would like to walk, and see that he is amused. When a young man is staying here it is not fair to leave him to fash himself being civil to an old woman like me, or reading books by himself in an attic. He has time enough alone in London to read, I am thinking."

"I believe he is fonder of talking to you than any other member of the family, grandma," replied Charlie, leaving the room.

He went upstairs, and found Caspar sitting on the sill of an open window, with a book in his lap. Charlie looked over his shoulder, and read:

"For love is as strong as death; jealousy is cruel as the grave; the coals thereof are coals of fire, which hath a most vehement flame. Many waters cannot quench love, neither can the floods drown it."

CHAPTER II.

THE DUTCH DEVIL.

MR. and Mrs. George Farringdon travelled to Paris, and their names were inscribed on the books of that luxurious and gigantic caravanserai called the Grand Hôtel du Louvre. They appeared at the *table d'hôte* pretty regularly, usually sitting in the same places, and became the nucleus of a small fortuitous concourse of very harmless good-natured English people, flavoured with an American admiral of indefinite age and quaint affectionately caustic tongue. They visited all the places and things which they ought to visit, they took drives and dined out of doors

in the various notable resorts within and beyond
the barriers, and were for a while extremely
happy and cheerful. George was still very
much in love with his wife, and was her un-
disputed and of course undisputable lord. To
be seen about with her was a cause of respect
and envy in others, and therefore of natural
exaltation in himself. And the sensation of
daily association with a lady of delicate tastes,
artistic tendency, personal beauty, and pleasant,
if sometimes rather incomprehensible dreamy
conversation, was new and grateful to him.
And he was grateful. He directed her to
choose, with the assistance and advice of the
best providers, a winter walking costume.
And when they left, when Paris grew cold
and windy, and drove its birds of passage
to rest and saunter in the Promenade des
Anglais, and watch the ceaseless lap of the
tideless sea, he was still undisturbed in the
belief that his wife was in love with him,

and regarded him as perhaps Undine regarded her knight. She might have been a fairy gift to him, to better and beautify his whole life, if he had only for a moment imagined her, or anyone else, capable of bettering or beautifying such a complete and satisfactory thing as he had hitherto found it. As for Dick herself, she was now nearer loving her husband, in the natural sense of the word, than she had ever been. She lived more in the present—a more wakeful life. Everyone was kind or good-natured to her, the world she lived in was bright, new, intelligent, and comfortable ; and destiny seemed to be shaping for her a placid, moderately happy life, untainted by high intellectual struggles or strong emotional influences. Something permanent of this kind was no doubt what she expected, when they started in the express, provided with Mann boudoir sleeping-cars, for the South.

Judging her husband as a moral thermometer, she had only noted his maximum register, and that not in the shade, or corrected to that sea-level which large human experience and time alone can teach.

The American admiral and a few other recently-found friends saw them off at the station. As the train started, the Admiral remarked to the little circle on the platform, as he cut off the end of an immense cigar : "Gingerbread's pretty as long as the gilt sticks on, ain't it?"

"How cynical you are, Admiral Sleaman!" observed a young English lady, still under the influence of that moon associated popularly with honey.

"How?"

"I do believe you are jealous of Mr. Farringdon."

"Maybe."

In a train, in the course of a long

journey, it is usual, after a decently prolonged suspicious silence, to make more or
less acquaintance with one's fellow-passengers.
Some people enter into conversation at once;
some—these being usually English—require
a trivial accident to loose the string of their
tongues; some require several hours' pre-
meditation, a custom-house and a collision.
But they will all talk ultimately if they are
given time. A few hours' travelling found
George Farringdon in conversation with the
one fellow-traveller in his compartment. He
spoke English well, but with a distinct
accent. He was a small man, quietly, but
well dressed, with a neatly-shaped head, very
close-cropped reddish hair, forming a point
on the forehead, narrow dark eyes, gold-
rimmed glasses, a rather beak-like nose, a
thin upper and a thick under lip, a small
waxed moustache, and a pointed chin. He
looked about thirty, but was probably younger.

His eyebrows had a trick of going up and down as he talked; in fact they were his principal gesticulatory apparatus. His face was rather long in proportion to its width, and had no definite expression. He seemed courteous and well informed. His conversation had a general and wide scope, such as any well-informed traveller might indulge in. He seemed well acquainted with France, or, at any rate, with the more frequented parts of it, as well as with London. He occasionally put an illustration or a quotation into his talk, which suggested some acquaintance with literature of an ordinary and generally-quoted kind. He seemed to possess a good deal of information about Nice, as well as about Monaco, and, having discovered that the Farringdons were visiting the former for the first time, ventured to recommend to them an hotel there—Beau Rivage, Bellevue, or some such name—which they saw no harm in trying, at any rate. They took refreshments together occasionally at such places on the way as afforded them the time and materials. The journey, of course, from Paris to Nice is long, and the best of scenery becomes wearisome after hours of railway motion, railway oscillation, and railway dirt, the latter working itself insidiously into the space between the neck and the collar, the wrist and sleeves, and making the hands unctuously gritty. So that the conversation in time languished from interest to commonplace, from commonplace to sleepy silence in cramped attitudes. On nearing the destination, all became brisker, however, and more confidential. The stranger stated that he was going to the before-mentioned hotel—call it Bellevue — and hoped he might frequently see them again. The Farringdons expressed a similar hope. Then the stranger asked if he might be allowed to introduce himself, and presented a card. It bore the name " Dr. Julius van Westerdijk."

" I am a Dutchman," he said, laughing; " but I am also all but a naturalised Englishman."

George Farringdon gave him his card gravely, and they parted at last for their several apartments, expressing mutual esteem. In fact, George invited him to join them at dinner; but Dr. Van Westerdijk delicately declined, saying he was sure, in their present tired state, they would rather be alone.

" Decent fellow, that," observed George. " First foreigner I've come across that I really like. But then he's half an Englishman really. Talks about the Park and the theatres like a native Londoner."

" He is very polite," said Dick, " and I see nothing against him; but I don't quite like his looks, somehow. I daresay it is quite an unreasonable fancy."

" Daresay." And they dined.

After a few long lazy sunny days, acquaintance ripened into intimacy, and George Farringdon spent a good deal of his spare time in the society of Dr. Van Westerdijk. They smoked cigarettes in the hotel smoking-room, and discussed the English papers and the hotel cookery. They walked about together, and drank beer in *cafés*. Even Dick thawed to the new friend, whom she now described as "the little Dutchman." Her attitude resembled that of the child who has been introduced to some strange animal—say a tame stoat—and has discovered, through daily association, that it apparently does not bite. Dr. Van Westerdijk allowed to leak out, in process of time, that he was the proprietor of the *Investigator* (a critical weekly paper dealing in literature, science, and art), which gained him respect in the English colony, and later, that he also owned *The Lamp*, which gained him much more respect, mingled with fear. People who had hitherto ignored his existence suddenly began to cultivate his acquaintance, and occasionally had their reward when they read in the paragraphic information, entitled " Flashes," their own names among those of such English visitors as were sufficiently exalted to deserve mention in a Society paper. George Farringdon was one of the first to receive that gratification, and his heart warmed to the small foreigner from that hour forward.

" Have you ever been over to that gaming-shop—what's its name—near here ? " said George one day, himself well knowing its name, having just finished reading a denunciatory article upon it in an English newspaper. They were sitting in the hotel courtyard, round a painted iron table supporting coffee and matches. George was on two chairs, Van Westerdijk on one. Dick was indoors, dressing to go out.

"Yes. Väi?"

"Is it as bad as they make out?"

"I do not know how bad tey make it out; but tey cannot paint it blacker tan it is."

"I mean all this business about suicides, and dropping fortunes in a few hours, and so on."

"It is done. Often. Tere was a man, a quäite yong man, vit a larch fortune, and a beautiful place in Wales, who went ofer tere and tropped te tam lot in tree tays. Last sômer. I knew him."

"Want of system, isn't it, makes a fellow lose?"

"Vant of money, as a rule. Yes. Do you mean to write an article on it?"

"No; not in my line, that, I'm afraid."

"Ah, now you vill excuse me if I say, do not you go tere to satisfy your own curiosity. I am an olter man tan you, and perhaps have seen a little more of te vorldt, and vot I say is, tone go! You have a väife—a sharming väife—and you are heir to a creat name and estate; you are young, you are prave, you are of te chivalric class. Tink of all tose responsibilities, and neffer mind te latics who will sharm you away, as the sirens tried to sharm Ulysses. Neffer mind te clang of te rouleau, te song of te Rhine daughters, or te ring of te Nibelung goldsmits. I have not offended you? No?"

"No, of course not, old fellow. Much obliged; but I think I know the world well enough by this time to take care of myself."

"If I hat not known tat I should not haf spoken. Tone go! Look at me! I neffer go."

Here Dick appeared, the one feature the garden missed, for no roses grew in it. She said, "Are you ready, George?"

"Yes." George tilted his brown hat forward from the nape of his neck, buttoned his brown coat, and stood upright.

Dr. Van Westerdijk had been standing ever since Dick appeared, bowing at intervals, his heels together.

"Do you know," she continued, "old Admiral Sleaman has come? I met him on the stairs."

"Oh, has he? Rum old boy; no harm in him."

"Contrariwise. And he has brought a curious-looking Irish friend with him from Paris, a patriot, the Admiral explained."

"Too patriotic to lif in Creat Pritain, perhaps, Madame Farringdon. Tat does occur."

"I don't know. I liked his face, though he did look rather 'fiery and untamed.'"

Enter Admiral Sleaman, U.S.N., and with him a robust gentleman with a tall hat on one side, black-rimmed eyeglasses, and a long grizzled red moustache.

"Glad to see you, Mr. Farringdon. Let me present my old friend Mr. Thaddeus O'Rourke — Mr. George Farringdon from England. What in anything's wrong with your friend?" Dr. Van Westerdijk had disappeared, with a greenish complexion beautifully "interpreted," as the critics say, by the colour of his fur—hair, that is to say—and a very unpleasant expression. He had blotted himself out. It was like the operatic scene where Mephistopheles cringes and dissolves as to his backbone before the crucial experiment of the sword-hilt. It is, perhaps, hardly fair to compare the little Doctor to Mephistopheles after his benevolent and thoughtful advice to George.

"Well, we are going out. Meet you at dinner, Admiral; and you, too, I hope, Mr. O'Rourke. Good-bye."

"Mr. Farringdon," began the Admiral.

"Yes."

"Who was that man?"

"A friend of mine—Dr. Van Westerdijk, proprietor of the *Investigator*, of which you may have heard."

"Ah!"

The Farringdons disappeared.

"O'Rourke."

"Sir."

"Mrs. Farringdon is quite a sweet young lady, is she not?"

"She is."

"I'm told Mr. Farringdon is a wealthy young man."

"I don't know."

"Who is Dr. Van What's-his-name, anyhow?"

"He is a blank sweep."

"Yes, he is so; snipe, we should say. What scared him?"

" My face. It has been frequently admired ; but he is prejudiced against it because
he saw it last through the disintegrating
works of a cane chair."

" How ? "

" I was breaking the same over his head."

" Good for you.   Have a cigar ? "

The Admiral produced two immense ones.
O'Rourke selected one.

" Say now, what do you know of that
complex result of inexplicable causes—that
Dutchman ? What's his game ? "

" Game of hawk and pigeon. Very old
game that."

" Here, waiter ! " added the Irishman to
one who happened to be passing.

" Sir."

" Do you know Dr. Van Westerdijk ?
Does he come here often ? "

" He has been here once or twice every
year for four years."

"Here, take this and go and take a drink. How does he make his money?"

"He gets some from England now. He has circular notes sent him. Changes them in the hotel."

"Any other way?"

"Of course. He is well known here as the Dutch Devil. Why? Because he always wins and never loses."

"Where?"

"At Monte Carlo. Where should it be?"

"Thank you."

After the paternal advice George Farringdon had received from Dr. Van Westerdijk, it is hardly necessary to explain that, as a man of the world who wishes to complete his mundane education, he took an early opportunity of visiting Monte Carlo. Nor is it, perhaps, necessary to add that he did not mention the fact to his wife or to anyone else. On the first visit nothing par-

ticular happened, and he came back with
the conviction that it was not half as
exciting or attractive as either its enemies
or its devotees made it out to be, and that
a quiet pool with fellows you know was far
more amusing. From the second visit he
came back a winner by a small amount,
bought a box of cigars, and came to the
conclusion that it was not bad fun after
all. From his sixth venture he returned in
the state generally known as " cleaned out."
He sought out Dr. Van Westerdijk, and
made a full and self-abasing confession to
that worthy, concluding with :

"And I'm hanged if I know how I'm
going to pay the hotel bill, to say nothing
of the journey back to England. I suppose
the police can't make them fork out? Of
course I know the whole thing's a swindle."

"No. The police will not gif you back
te money you trow away, onless you can

proof it to be a sevindle, and tat is not likely. 'Ow much to you want?"

George, on whose despondent heart a ray of light now shone, mentioned a sum.

"All tat? I can pay your hotel bill and your tickets if you laike. Yes? But I am too poor for the rest."

"My dear fellow, I couldn't think— you're awfully good, you know; but really, could you advance me a little ready?"

"In te first place, tone go to any of te professional money-lenders here; tey are worse tan Monte Carlo. I advaise you to go back to England. When you are in London, you go to tis address; take my card wit you—tey are friends of mine—it is a firm of honest merchants who may help you. No; I forgot."

"What?" George was being alternately raised and depressed, as a fish that is played, or a pipe that is played on.

"I tink tey tislike advancing money. Tey to not wish to be compared to te common Shews and sevindlers."

"Couldn't it be managed somehow? Do think of some dodge."

"You shall have a note from me, and I will ask it as a particular fafor to me. Peraps tey will ten to someting."

"You are a good fellow, Van Westerdijk, and I'm awfully lucky to have met you."

"Lockier still if you had tekken my advice."

"I say."

"Vell?"

"Don't talk about these things when you are with my wife, will you? She wouldn't understand, you know."

"Of course."

George wrung his hand and disappeared. The little "Dutch Devil" skipped fantastically round the smoking-room, snapping a rude air on his fingers, and then looked nervously out of the window to see if he had been observed. He then sat down, lit a cigarette, drew a sheet of note-paper to him, and wrote as follows:

" MADAME,

"The young man is going to England. He goes to M. & Co. Let them be ready.

"I kiss your hands, and hope to see you soon again.—Your most humble servant,

"VAN WESTERDIJK."

"Kiss your hands! I'll kiss your face yet, madame!" he muttered. "Genius," he observed in his own tongue to the empty chairs, " claims higher rewards than expenses and commission. I am not a machine to be satisfied with coals and occasional oiling. I am a creature of emotions, and my emotions centre in one object; at least they have done lately, since our first interview a few months ago, gracious Empress of Weissnichtwo. You with your face, with what is rarer—your brain—behind it, your passions behind that, allied to me with my brains, my manners, my education, and my influence—Lord of Abraham, what a partnership! You want a master to direct your powers; none could fill the place like me. I will be your master; I, Doctor of Philosophy of Leyden, I swear it!"

"Mr. Farringdon, sir," said Admiral Sleaman, "that Dutch friend of yours is a snipe. Let him 'alone. Excuse me, but that is so."

"Excuse me, Admiral, but I prefer to choose my friends for myself, and have reason to count Dr. Van Westerdijk among my best," replied George haughtily.

CHAPTER III.

A FRIENDLY ALLIANCE.

AFTER the wedding at Sokebridge, Kimburls and his sister took their leave of Claudius, and were conveyed in a train to distant Glasgow, to the great relief of their distinguished host, who had latterly found their presence almost maddening, unrelieved by that of the younger generation, and thrown unrestrictedly on his resources of entertainment. They diverted him to the last moment with long wrangles on routes and "Bradshaw," which exciting treatise they studied and discussed together, becoming extremely warm and dishevelled over it before arriving at a definite issue of distinct mutual contra-

diction, at which juncture they appealed to
Claudius as umpire. The latter —whose
notion of travelling was to put his hat on
and start when Alphonse told him the carriage was ready; to get into the train when
Alphonse told him it was time, and that the
tickets were procured, the carriage warmed,
and the newspapers cut; to get out when
Alphonse told him the destination was reached
and a cab waiting—was not of much assistance to them, until the idea occurred to
him : "I must put these creatures in charge
of Alphonse, and tell him not to come into
my sight again till he can certify that they
are in a fast train which does not stop for
thirty miles from here." He therefore offered
the assistance of his servant, who was used
to travelling. They accepted, and the result
was that in half-an-hour's time they were
at the station ; in two hours they were in
London. Claudius was very nearly carried
away by his feelings into doing an eccentric

saraband round his library when they drove
away. He very nearly fell over various
things, subsided into his armchair, and
ecstatically lit his largest, curliest, deepest-
coloured meerschaum. That afternoon Mrs.
Brandon arrived, having been, Claudius pre-
sumed, in London all the time. After a
short conversation, in which Claudius told
her all his troubles and experiences of the
last few days, she said :

"And what has become of the young
couple ? "

"Paris, pictures, dresses, shop-visiting in
broken English, ices—you know."

"Indeed ! Where shall I forward Mr.
George Farringdon's letters ? "

"Hôtel du Louvre. Now let's drop that
subject."

"Very well. Shall I read you something ? "

"If you will be so kind. Here is this
rather recent French book that has attracted

a lot of attention, the papers say, ' Le Nabab.' Do you know it ? "

" Yes ; I'd like to read it again. There's a character in it I should think you would admire—the Duc de Mora. Where's the book?"

"Here you are. Make yourself comfortable, take forty cigarettes and a matchbox into your lap, and drive ahead."

" Your Excellency shall be obeyed."

That evening Mrs. Brandon wrote a note and posted it herself. It was as follows:

" DEAR DR. VAN WESTERDIJK,

" If you think of visiting Paris I should recommend you to go to the Louvre. It is well worth seeing. Mr. N. R. will gladly give you letters of recommendation to his friends the bankers, Steinthal & Schloss, Rue Vivienne. I enclose photograph as per desire. It is a good likeness.

" Yours very truly,

"J. BRANDON."

The only curious thing about this note was that the photograph enclosed was not of herself. It was George Farringdon's. Three days later came a post-card from Paris, with two or three words in a strange tongue, which read from right to left. She smiled pleasantly and threw it in the fire. It amused her to wonder what the bright eyes of monkey-faced Alphonse had made of this when he laid the breakfast and scanned the correspondence.

"At the same time," she reflected, "this is absurdly theatrical of him. It is rather like the half-educated political conspirator, who reveres symbolic red caps, and skulls, and bowls of blood. He might just as well have written in good English and put it in an envelope. Ah! but he has saved fifteen centimes by this means. I forgot that. He is scrupulous with our money, we are to understand, I suppose. He is a clever little man—I rather like him. I don't believe he could deceive me—or that he would try."

The mysterious inscription only meant "I have known him," and implied, no doubt, that Van Westerdijk had used the photograph sent him for the purpose of identifying its owner. As we know, he did not make any effort to make the young Farringdons' acquaintance until they started for Nice. He spent the rest of the time in amusing himself in Paris, as he could very readily afford to do, with the combined assistance of the profits of two serial papers, the letters to Steinthal & Schloss, and an occasional little stroke of "business" of one kind and another. In what he called "business" the little Doctor walked apart and was peculiar, and his ways were past finding out. It may be that he was particularly lucky at games of chance, such as the Bourse, or games of skill, such as billiards. It may have been both or neither, for all his acquaintances ever succeeded in discovering. Whatever it was, it seemed to prosper.

In the meantime Caspar stayed on with

the Deanes through the early autumn, becoming more and more of a general favourite
in that house. Sometimes he would go with
Charlie and Lily in a boat, and pull or sail
"round the cape," as Lily called the journey
by water out of Sokebridge Bay into its next
neighbour Barstone Bay; and they would rest
on their oars in the still September evenings
out on that placid sea, and all look out to the
shoreless west, where the clouds were in alter-
nate orange and smoky streaks stretching over
miles and lonely miles of horizon. And they
would turn then to the sun-streaked angles
and promontories of the brown and yellow
earthy cliffs, which bore on their shoulders
the little town, with its red roofs coming here
and there through some cleft or depression
into the sight of the gazers on the water far
below. Sometimes, again, they would go out
for long walks, through woods and over downs,
till Caspar quite learned the geography of the
neighbourhood, and began to wonder why

people who lived in the country ever cared to leave it. He and Miss Deane had long and amusing discussions in the evenings, beginning usually with literature, and ending with things in general. She and he each wrote a story against one another and against time. He read his aloud, by request, and amused and surprised them with it, and then insisted on Miss Deane's being read. This was done against all protest by Charlie, and both stories were inserted, to the great delight of the whole Deane family, in the *Lamp*, to whose staff Caspar had succeeded in attaching himself.

To Lily Carew he was the object of special interest and curiosity. He was, she thought, a riddle to which she knew the answer. She had guessed, with the help of Charlie's Schlangenberg letter, at a state of things which never entered the dreams of the elder branch of the family. Much as they liked Caspar, he had many moods and strange sayings and looks, for which they were unable to supply reasons. It came into Lily's head that she had the opening chapters of a complicated and rather enthralling romance before her, to which she— and perhaps Charlie—alone had the paper-knife, as it were. He was reticent and laconic whenever the Farringdons became the subject of conversation, as, of course, often happened, and said nothing which suggested any special interest in them on his part. All the more reason, argued this female detective and psychologist, for taking all that was unsaid for granted. She had a taste for mysteries and romances (was she not an author?) and here was her opportunity for mixing in one, in some capacity or other. She resolved that she was competent to take upon herself the office of interrogator and repository of confidences.

Accordingly, one fine afternoon, when her grandmother was dozing over her knitting, her aunt out shopping, and Charlie engaged in reading up the accelerator and depressor nerves in his room, she found Caspar pacing moodily about the lawn with a pipe in his mouth, no hat on his head, and a volume of German poetry in his hands, and spake to him as follows:

"You'll get a sunstroke, Mr. Rosenfeld!"

"Ah, you, is it?" And Caspar's face brightened. He liked the pretty and wayward little brunette, as one cannot help liking anything lively, pretty, and I nearly said harmless; but it is unsafe to make assertions which events may disprove.

"It is me—I, I mean. I am going into the kitchen-garden, not to pick a cabbage to make an apple-pie of, but to eat gooseberries and black currants. Will you come and have some? You had better, or I shall take them all and be very ill, and it will be your fault."

"Yes, I will come. Don't depend on me for the eating, though."

And they strolled off.

"Don't you like black currants?"

"When I was your age I didn't have the chance of getting any. Now I don't care much for them. We are Time's fools."

"What were you reading when I came?"

"A sort of story about a poor trumpeter, who made songs in exile about the land he left behind him, about the old home, and how heavy it made his heart, and a good deal more to that effect, with elucidations by a very acute old cat."

"Tell me more about it; translate some."

"These orders are very sudden; I don't know exactly which you would like."

"Begin with the one you were reading when I interrupted you."

"In English it is something like this:

This is of all life's cruel wrongs the wrongest,
   That fairest rose-buds bear the thorns of pain;
That in all love, the shortest and the longest,
   We meet at first, at last to part again.

You will understand that it is quite against my principles to translate. It is fatal to this kind of German verse."

"Never mind, go on."

> For in your eyes I think I once have seen
>   A light like love, that lit the night in me.
> God help you! dreaming of what might have been;
>   God shield you! for it was too good to be.

"I can't get any further, I don't think, without muddling it worse."

"Why do you read that melancholy stuff?"

"Why do you eat black currants?"

"That is a comparison I had not thought of making. I don't think that book agrees with you half as well as they do with me."

"Don't you? Why not?"

"Because you are always reading it when you are by yourself, and you look gloomy and solemn—like Hamlet. Then you are very cheerful with us, and talk a great deal of nonsense when there is any one to listen, like Hamlet. So I think you must have something on your mind, also like him."

" Dear me ! What else have you been pleased to notice ? "

" Only one other thing which has any connection with your solemnity, and your striding about with a German book and without a hat—you will really get softening of the brain if you don't get a hat."

" Like Hamlet, you would add ? "

" No. I used to think he was mad, because I was told so; but if I did, I daren't say it now before you."

" Well, what is this other thing you have noticed? Symptoms that my brain is becoming what Galen says most brains are —merely a spongy gland ? "

" You won't be offended, if I tell you ? "

" No, not visibly."

" Promise."

" By the nine gods I swear ! What was it ? "

"Your expression when Dick Farringdon passed you on her way to the altar."

"Eh!" said Caspar suddenly, in a different and deeper voice. "What did you see then?"

"Oh, I'm not good at describing! You know what I mean. I'm awfully sorry if I've annoyed you."

"No—no—no," replied Caspar absently and slowly; "I did not think I was so transparent."

"I like her so much," said Lily, with a girl's tact for saying the right thing when she chooses.

"Do you, Miss Carew? Then I think she has got a good friend."

"Is that sarcastic?"

"No; not the least."

"I thought the whole thing, wedding and all that, such a hateful pity. I never liked him."

Caspar said naught.

"Mr. Rosenfeld, girls can do things and understand things that men can't always. You may think me an awful young fool, but I do think sometimes. I wanted to tell you I would stick to Dick Farringdon, if I could be any good to her, whatever happened to her. I know something will happen to her; and I don't care what people say, you know, as long as I get my way. So remember, I shall always be her friend, and ready to do anything for her. I thought you would like to know this when you are away by yourself working in London, and she should be here, perhaps. I like her more than any girl I ever saw. Don't you? Oh, I beg your pardon!"

"Lily Carew, I can only say thank you. I am very glad you told me this; though how on earth you come to know so much about it——"

"About you, you mean! Oh, I'm a witch—a black witch."

"I think you are. We'll burn you some day; say next 5th of November."

"Now, that *is* unkind, after all my

trouble.   This is all private and confidential, of course, Mr. Rosenfeld ? "

" Certainly."

And thence a firm alliance was ratified, which remained firm, for all the flouts and jeers which were usually exchanged before an audience, between Lily Carew, the English waif from Spanish America, and Caspar Rosenfeld, the Jew.

Some weeks after this, on looking over the paragraphic " Flashes " in a copy of *The Lamp*, Caspar was surprised to read that Mr. and Mrs. Malcolm Farringdon had arrived at Nice, and were staying at the Bellevue Hotel.

" How on earth do they get in here ? " was his reflection.

THE END OF VOL. II.

CHARLES DICKENS AND EVANS, CRYSTAL PALACE PRESS.